THE CAPTAIN'S MATE

THE BLUE SOLACE: BOOK SIX

C.W. GRAY

❀ Created with Vellum

Draif and Lucas's story begins at the same time as the events in *The Engineer's Mate*. As Beck and Beol are falling in love and dealing with the Bracken, Draif is researching the leaders of Humans First and working closely with the Lord Admiral to decide how to deal with the specieist organization.

ANCHORS REST SYSTEM, CHARYBDIS
STATION

"Dottie, I can't thank you enough for your contact list," Draif Ando said, smiling at the older woman on the screen in front of him. Her wild and tangled gray hair stuck up in all directions from the wind that blew through the spaceport on Vextonar.

Dottie was a bit crazy and a bit evil mastermind, but she had a heart as big as the galaxy and had been one of the few to really *see* him when he'd lived on Vextonar. There had been more than a few times her strong arms had held him as he cried. Her strange, mixed-up scent of ship fumes and basil was as familiar to him as the scars on his face.

Draif cleared his throat, chasing away the nostalgia. "Each person you introduced me to has been helpful in hunting down the information I need. A few even sent me on to some of their own contacts."

Dottie's wide grin lit up her eyes. "Good. It took me years to find them, but they're good and talented folks. I know you'll treat them right."

Draif grinned. "They like my money just as much as yours. I'm putting my pieces in place, and we'll catch Humans First unawares."

Her body shook with her laugh. "I knew the first time we met you were a sneaky bastard, kiddo. You remind me of an Old-Earth bird I read about. Black Herons would hunt fish in the shallows by spreading their wings over one spot and tricking the fish into thinking it was night. The poor fish would poke their heads up, believing they were safe, and the Black Heron would eat them up."

"I'll do my best to take HF down," Draif said, nodding. "They're arrogant fuckers. I don't think they understand what they're getting into."

Dottie looked sad for a moment. "It's getting bad here, kiddo. Vextonar has always been specieist, but the government and the Prime are pushing harder and harder each day. They want a planet of pureblood humans."

Draif frowned. "There are no pureblood humans anymore. Besides, the Prime like their slaves and servants. How does that fit?"

She shrugged. "I didn't say they were making sense, Draify. I think that's what scares me the most. It's like something is stirring the pot just to see it boil over."

"It has to be Humans First. We'll deal with it."

Dottie smiled softly. "You're a good boy, Draif. Did you know that Lord Admiral of yours personally called me up to thank me for sending you and Leti to them?"

Draif scratched his ear. "Oh, well, Fasi loves Leti. He's married to Fasi's son, after all."

She arched a brow. "We all love Leti, Draif, but we love you too. You're a good addition to the station, and Lord Admiral Juren knows it. Don't sell yourself short, kiddo."

Draif didn't know how to respond. He knew people put up with him for Leti's sake, and he tried to be as helpful as possible, but love was a completely different thing.

A beeping sound came through from Dottie's end, and she groaned. "Okay. Our secure line is breaking. Take care, kiddo. Give them hell."

Their call ended, and Draif stared at the blank screen as he thought about all the pieces moving around him. Dottie had handed over her network of hackers, smugglers, and spies. The woman liked to know what was happening in the galaxy. Draif felt like he was becoming Charybdis Station's Dottie – a very inferior Dottie.

An alert pinged on his tablet, and he looked it over. Stocks in the production company had risen like he thought they would. *Time to sell a few stocks.* A few clicks later, and he checked his account. *Yes!*

He looked up from the screen of his tablet when his chubby, orange tabby cat hopped on his bed. Marmalade *meowed*, then begin kneading the soft bed beside him, intent on making the perfect napping spot.

He smiled softly, the scars on his cheeks tightening. "We made a lot of credits today, Marmalade. It was a good choice to buy into that company, and I think we'll make even more later on."

Marmalade circled twice, then settled into a large ball against his leg.

"We'll put what we made today in our savings, then look into that new start-up on Derelict."

Marmalade ignored him and started purring. She was a constant warm comfort against his leg.

Draif started to dig into the company a bit. It looked like a start-up shipping company, which would do a lot of good for the merchant world. The CEO was a young human with a large guardian fleet to escort his ships. He promised a safe and timely delivery, and so far, that's what he provided.

Draif's eyes narrowed as he read Gus's report on the man. "Oh, Mr. Chad Ige, aren't you interesting?"

"What are you plotting in here?"

Draif looked up at Lucas's words. His friend leaned against the doorframe. The man was a Betonize-Cardinal hybrid with a pair of silky-brown ears atop his head and a matching furry tail just like a Cardinal. His fangs, dark eyes, and large size were all Betonize.

One of his eyes had a slightly silver sheen to it when the light hit it right. He'd lost the eye when he'd lost his leg and arm.

Draif pressed a hand to his chest, trying to steady the frantic beats of his heart. Recently, he'd started noticing the width of Lucas's shoulders and the controlled and graceful way he moved as he walked. It was a problem.

"Well," Lucas asked. "What are you up to?"

"Researching a guy – Chad Ige, CEO of that shipping company I was telling you about."

"What did you find?"

"Company is legit and looks like a good investment. The man is smart and doesn't take anyone's shit. I like him."

Lucas's ears flattened, and his tail swished in irritation behind him.

"I think he might be a useful asset," Draif said. "My contact says he despises Humans First, even if he isn't public about it. I'll contact my guy and get him digging into him."

Lucas's tail stopped swishing, and his ears perked back up. "Useful asset, huh?"

Draif winced. "I shouldn't think of a person like that. This thing with Humans First is messing with my head. All I can think about is taking them down."

Well, that and you, he thought. Lately, his dreams had been all about his friend. He'd dreamed of Lucas holding him, kissing him, even fucking him.

He made a face. Friends didn't think of friends that way.

Lucas slipped onto the bed and settled down next to him.

Draif almost swore. Damn if Lucas didn't make things worse.

Even a month ago, it wouldn't have bothered him a bit to sit on the bed with Lucas and Marmalade. They often watched vids and talked before bedtime. There had been many nights when they'd fallen asleep together.

Hell, Lucas still lived with Draif. It had started as a way to keep an eye on his friend as Lucas adjusted to the robotic prosthesis he had needed for his left leg and right arm. Then, after he was healed and adjusted to his new limbs, Lucas just never left.

He had his own room next to Draif's and had done a lot more to make this huge house a home than Draif ever could.

"Humans First need to be taken down, but you don't have to do it alone," Lucas said, leaning over to bump him with his shoulder.

Draif gave him a half-smile and dipped his head, letting his long hair fall over his face. "I know. I just have all these ideas and want to see if they play out. It's like a game of chess, and I fucking love it. Then I feel bad for getting excited about this. If we're right about them, they've killed billions of people."

Lucas considered him for a moment before smiling, his sharp fangs gleaming. "I sure as shit love fighting, but that doesn't mean I enjoy wars. If I never killed another person for as long as I lived, I'd be perfectly happy. You enjoy the intrigue of this. I think if you weren't focused on HF, you'd probably be focused on something else, like improving the station's security measures."

Draif felt the little ball of worry that had been stuck in his chest for days start to loosen. Lucas and Draif's best friend, Leti, had a way of making his worries disappear.

"You're right." Draif tapped out a message to Dottie's favorite hacker, Gus. The man was damn good and had somehow become Draif's friend. The man also liked the idea of taking down HF.

Lucas stroked Marmalade's rolled-up form. "You shouldn't spend your whole day off working on your tablet. Your hair keeps falling in your face. Do you want to go get it cut? I know it bugs you when you're sparring."

Draif's stomach rumbled. "Why don't we get lunch at Juniper's? I'm starving."

Lucas smiled, and the dimple in his right cheek almost made Draif groan. "Good idea."

A few moments later, they were ready and walking toward the diner.

Draif kept his eyes on his tablet as they walked. "What are we doing tomorrow? I was thinking that maybe we could get Anders, Crimson, and Ned together for some training. Selene's been spending time with the Half Moon people. I want to see what they can do, and our crew could use the workout."

Draif felt Lucas's hands on his shoulders as his friend steered him toward the diner. He tried not to shiver at Lucas's touch.

"That's a good idea. We could do a morning session if the Guild Master is alright with it."

Draif cleared his throat. "I'll check with him."

A high-pitched, annoying voice grabbed Draif's attention. "Lucas!" An attractive Cardinal woman with rich chestnut ears and hair ran toward them.

"Fuck," Draif said quietly. "Again?"

Lucas shot him an apologetic look and caught the woman when she threw herself in his arms. "Hi, Ginger. It's been a while."

"Years," she squealed and hugged him tighter. "Ever

since you joined with Blue Solace, we never see you out at the clubs or bars."

"He's been busy," Draif said shortly.

This wasn't the first time an attractive person put hands all over Lucas in public. Apparently, he was quite the partier before joining Hack's crew.

It didn't use to bother him, but since a few months ago, the touchy-feely, slightly groping behavior of Lucas's fans grated on his nerves. It happened every couple of weeks. They would be in the midst of walking down the street, eating at the diner, or training with the crew and some stranger would run up and touch Lucas. It was so fucking annoying.

Lucas was *his* lieutenant. They had no right to just grab him.

Ginger eyed the burns on Draif's face before dismissing him. "Where have you been, Lucas? We still see Finn and Juniper around, but you've been elusive."

"He's not a wildebeest to be hunted," Draif said, voice hard.

Ginger huffed. "Who're you?"

"The captain of the Blue Raven," Draif said, smirking and waving her away. "Lucas is busy right now. Run along."

Lucas snorted. "We really do need to go. Talk to you later, Ginger."

The woman glared at Draif as they walked away.

Draif forced himself not to make a face at the woman. "How many fuckbuddies do you have?"

Lucas almost choked on a laugh. "Damn, Draif.

First, they aren't fuckbuddies, just friends. Second, why does it matter?"

Draif shrugged. "It doesn't. I'm just curious."

Lucas gave him a look. "Curious?"

"We run into them all the damn time."

"I have lots of *friends*, Draif." Lucas nudged him with his shoulder. "Haven't slept with anyone since we met."

Draif's eyes widened. "Seriously? That's a long time. I didn't know normal men could go that long without sex."

Lucas arched a brow. "Normal?"

Draif flushed. "A normal sex drive."

"There isn't a *normal* sex drive," Lucas said, rolling his eyes. "There's only *your own* sex drive. There's nothing wrong with you."

Draif growled. "I never said there was."

"You were implying it. There's nothing wrong with being demisexual."

"Anyway," Draif said. "We were talking about you."

Lucas grinned. "If we can't talk about your sex life, then we can't talk about mine."

Draif huffed. "Lucas."

Lucas sighed dramatically. "Draif."

They arrived at Juniper's diner before Draif could think of something to say.

Juniper's chicken, Ms. Speckles, sat in her favorite flower pot and clucked at people as they passed. Hector, a fat rooster, walked around her flower pot protectively, pecking at the grass between glaring at people.

"Looks like Dannol is in," Lucas said, nodding at the rooster. "Hey, Hector. Nice day, isn't it?"

Draif laughed. "Does the rooster talk back?"

"Ha, ha, ha," Lucas said dryly and pushed Draif through the door.

The diner was as busy as usual. Several members of the Blue Fleet frequented the place, but there were still a few people from other sectors in the station.

Juniper waved at them from behind the bar. "Go sit with Cas, guys. The place is busy, and I need to keep tables open."

Draif shared a look with Lucas. "Don't you feel loved? He doesn't even want to give us a table of our own."

"Come and sit," Cas called out from his table against one of the back windows.

The large blue Grell sat with his friend and fellow general Audre.

Draif nodded to them and sat, eyeing the various pets that ran around the backyard of the diner. "Why is Pork Chop dressed like a... pork chop?"

Audre snorted. "Only Juniper understands that one."

"Hey guys," Juniper said, breathing a little hard. "What can I get you?"

Draif frowned. "Do you need some help?"

Juniper bit his lip. "If you'll refill those drinks in the back-corner booth, I'll give you lunch for free. There's twelve of them, and I'm barely keeping up here since it's just Remy and me on the floor."

"On it," Draif said, hopping up. "Lucas can order for me."

He grabbed a few pitchers and headed toward the table. He almost turned around when he saw who was there.

Most of the people on Charybdis Station had accepted him with open arms. It helped that it was well known he was a friend of the Lord Admiral. There were times, though, that the occasional person liked to remind him of his *place*.

Three particular captains in the Blue Fleet stood out the most – Captains Yeardley, Wyther, and Reed. The three captains, their lieutenants, weapons specialists, and three strangers sat at the large curved booth.

Yeardley's eyes widened. "Damn it, Ando. Captains don't wait tables in a diner. What will your crew think?"

"Just refilling your drinks for Juniper," Draif said.

"You need to focus on your training," Wyther said, face solemn. "From bed-slave to a ship's captain in less than two years is shit. No one should expect you to captain a ship without the proper training."

One of the strangers gaped. "Bed-slave? With that face?"

Wyther glared at the woman. "Doesn't matter what he looks like. He's a free man."

Another of the strangers looked around nervously. "The Lord Admiral wouldn't have made him a captain if he wasn't capable."

Reed's hard eyes watched him as he refilled their

drinks. "It takes skill to captain a ship, Ando. You should be in the pile of soldiers training every day, sitting in on the diplomacy and strategy classes, and working with your crew."

Draif filled up the last cup. "It's just all so hard. There's so many forms to fill out, and the crew keep bugging me about things."

Yeardley gave him a sympathetic look. "Maybe you should get your lieutenant more involved. I hear he's a good fighter. He can at least train your crew."

Draif gasped, trying not to overdo it. "That's a really good idea. Thanks, Captain Yeardley. Have a good meal, everyone."

He turned on his heel and gave an annoyed huff when he sat at his table.

Cas's brows rose. "What's wrong?"

Lucas looked over at the table and cursed. "Those asshats bothering you again?"

"Someone's bothering you?" Audre started to stand.

"Sit down," Draif said, unable to stop his laugh. "It's my business to handle."

Lucas scowled. "They think Draif is an idiot and keep trying to get him to either train harder or give up captaining the ship."

Cas snorted and stood. "Dipshits. Let's kick their asses."

"Yes!" Lucas jumped up.

"Sit down," Draif said again, rolling his eyes. "They're entitled to their opinions. It's annoying, but I'll deal with it."

Lucas groaned as he fell back into his seat. "You just like to play with them."

Cas pouted but also sat. "It's stupid. Hack and Dad aren't going to make anyone a captain if they don't deserve it. For fuck's sake, you can kick my ass in sparring and strategizing."

"They only see your accomplishments," Audre said thoughtfully, tapping her chin. "Not the work it took you to get there."

"I tried to explain my training background, but they thought I was lying," Draif said.

Cas shook his head. "The way Dad and Mom talk about you should convince anyone. They shouldn't have to see you struggling on the sparring mats."

Draif smiled softly. He greatly respected Fasi and Renee Juren. They were good people and had made him feel like part of their family. He knew that was part of the reason he was so determined to solve the puzzle that was Humans First.

He wanted Fasi and Renee to be proud of him. He wanted to be worthy of Charybdis Station and Lucas.

"Before joining Charybdis Station, Yeardley was a member of the Rutbuk Mercenary group. Because she's a mixed-hybrid and looks so delicate, she was passed over for promotion to captain several times," Draif said. "According to my sources, two of the men that were promoted before her were incompetent assholes who ended up getting their crews killed. Yeardley, however, is a good captain. She's practical and can get the job done without making a spectacle."

Cas, Audre, and Lucas stared at him.

"Wyther is Drellian and his family deals in slavery, but he can't stand it. He set out to make his own fortune and joined Charybdis Station because he liked that we made money but acted with honor. It took him seven years to get his own ship, and he's more than earned it."

Lucas blinked. "How do you know all of this?"

Draif shrugged. "It would be stupid not to know my enemy. Anyway, Reed's family has been a part of Charybdis Station for six generations. They were one of the first Grell families to settle on the station. He's an excellent captain, but a childhood friend of his died under his watch and he's felt guilty about it for years. He's protective of the station and every single citizen."

Audre shook her head. "Do you have full dossiers on them?"

Draif gave her an innocent look. "I don't know what you're talking about."

"It doesn't matter," Cas said, looking upset. "They're captains in the same fleet as you. You shouldn't have to prove that you earned your place once you have Dad and Hack's approval. No person here should have to do that."

"I do," Draif said softly. "Each of those captains have legitimate concerns. Their worries are coming from a good place, as annoying as they are."

Audre's expression hardened. "The leadership of Charybdis Station knows and trusts you. That should be enough."

"Don't worry," Draif said. "They may not know me yet, but they will."

2

*L*ucas leaned against the wall and typed out a message to Ginger. *No thanks. I have plans, but I'll see you around.*

Draif and Bendix circled one another in the Half Moon training room as Draif's crew and several assassins watched.

You never turned down a Havenite party before. Is it that scarred guy?

Lucas scowled. Draif's scars weren't even that noticeable, but it was still a shit thing to point out or bring up.

That scarred guy is my best friend. Fuck off.

Bendix was a big guy but moved well. He strolled around the edges of the mat, completely nonchalant. Draif, on the other hand, moved nervously, hand fidgeting. He bit his lip and watched Bendix with narrowed eyes.

Lucas grinned. *Sneaky faker.*

His communicator chirped again. *What the hell,*

Lucas? We've been friends for years and you tell me to fuck off?

Lucas huffed. He had more important shit to do than placate a woman he hadn't seen or talked to in years. He'd had a lot of friends before joining Blue Solace, but they were all surface friends – there for a good time and little else. He had thought Ginger had more depth, but it looked like he was wrong.

Draif is a good man and you reduce him to 'that scarred guy.' Again. Fuck off.

Otto, a Half Moon assassin, shook his head and winced when Draif swallowed hard and aimed a kick at Bendix. It was fast and hard, but a green recruit would have seen it coming.

Bendix blocked the kick and grabbed Draif's leg. "Seriously?"

Draif moved, smooth as water, falling to the mat and pushing into Bendix's hold. A quick jab to the man's balls freed his leg, and another quick spinning kick knocked the large assassin to the mat.

Almost instantly, Draif straddled his chest and had a small blade at Bendix's throat.

Ned, one of Draif's soldiers, whooped. "Damn right, Captain."

"Point to Draif," Otto said, grinning. "But it's not over yet."

Bendix grabbed Draif's wrist and rolled. Then, they were just a blur of movement. Bendix got in a jab to Draif's side but received a solid hit in his solar plexus, causing him to fall back.

"Another point to Draif," Anders, Draif's weapons specialist, said. "Kick his ass, Captain!"

"Come on, Bendix! Show him what you got," Otto yelled, then laughed when Bendix hit the mat again. "Do you need help?"

Lucas laughed at the glare Bendix shot his friend.

His comm chimed again. *I'm sorry. Captain Draif Ando of the Blue Raven is important to you, huh?*

Lucas smiled softly. There was the Ginger he remembered. *Yeah. Apology accepted.*

I was jealous. We haven't seen each other in ages, and I wanted to just pick up where we left off. Now, I'll just be happy to catch up with you. AS FRIENDS! Tell your territorial captain that so he doesn't hunt me down.

Lucas read the message thoughtfully. Draif had been a lot more hostile with Ginger than some of Lucas's other acquaintances. He'd been acting odd the last few months.

Since you clearly asked around about him, what did the gossip mill say?

Your captain has an 'in' with the Lord Admiral and General Hackett. He's important folk, but some don't like it. He may have earned the leadership's respect, but his peers are doubtful.

What about you?

I'm not stupid. No one gets a ship at Charybdis Station unless they've more than proved themselves. Plus, he has your complete loyalty. It's been a while, Lucas, but I remember you.

Draif spun around Bendix's body and put the large man in a chokehold. Damn, the man was good.

We can meet for dinner at Juniper's. I live with Draif, and neither of us like cooking.

You live together? It's like that, is it?

Not yet, but hopefully one day.

I'll see you at the diner.

"I give," Bendix said, groaning from where he lay on the mat. "You win."

Draif narrowed his eyes. "Not yet. Stop holding back, big guy."

Otto blinked. "Holding back? Were you holding back, Bendix?"

Bendix scowled. "Kind of. We're in front of his crew."

Draif punched him in the face. Straight on and hard. "No holding back."

Shit. Things just got real. Have to go make sure my captain doesn't kill someone.

"Uh, Draif," Lucas said when the two men began to fight in earnest. "Oh, another kick to the balls."

This fight was dirtier and rougher than the first. Bendix got in a lot more hits, but by the end, he was still the one pinned on the mat.

The man croaked out a laugh. "You fucking bit me! I give. For real this time."

Draif hopped up, breathing heavily as he looked around at the crowd. "Ready to start training?"

They all groaned but gathered around. For the next two hours, Draif, Lucas, and the assassins worked with Anders, Crimson, and Ned.

"Ned, you're getting better, but don't hesitate to go for the groin, eyes, or knees," Lucas said. "Your goal is to stay alive, down your opponent, and move on to the next. Fighting dirty isn't something to be avoided."

Bendix leaned down and adjusted Ned's stance. "How the fuck do you think Draif kicked my ass? We aren't dueling here. Anything goes in a fight, be it a battle or a sparring match."

Lucas nodded at the assassin and left Ned in his care. Draif trained with Crimson, another one of their soldiers, while Anders and Otto faced off on the mat.

Moyra, one of Half Moon's top assassins, made her way to his side, dark skin gleaming in the light. "Your man has some nice moves, lovely Lucas."

He groaned. "Stop calling me that."

She shrugged and grabbed his ears. "Can't help it. I think it's these ears. They're so cute."

Lucas heard a deep growl, then Moyra yelped as she was picked up and thrown over Draif's shoulder.

Draif scowled and carried her to the mat. "Don't touch him!"

Moyra looked up from where she was draped and gave Lucas a delighted look.

Lucas shook his head. "Captain, what's going on?"

Draif set the assassin down. "Moyra is going to work with Crimson on his hand-to-hand skills."

She surprised Draif with a tight hug. "Sure I am, Captain Cranky."

Draif grabbed Lucas's arm. "Come on. Let's spar."

———

LATER THAT NIGHT, LUCAS FOUND HIMSELF IN A SMALL

booth against the window of Juniper's diner. Ginger sat across from him.

Her brown eyes were full of mischief. "How did your captain take the news that you were meeting me for dinner?"

Lucas sighed. "He was pissed. I don't get it. I've met friends for a meal several times since we've known each other, and he's never gotten mad before. He's been acting strange lately."

"Hmm. How's he been acting?"

"He's hostile to anyone that touches me. We don't talk as much anymore. It's almost like he's feeling shy or self-conscious. He hides his face behind his hair anytime he notices me looking at him. Then, there's the fact that he's always fidgeting. He seems uncomfortable when he's alone in the same room with me."

"He wasn't always like this?"

"No. We've been friends for a while now. He's always been comfortable in his own skin and driven to be the best at any- and everything. The things that man can do are amazing. Then, he would talk to me about our lives, our pasts, what we wanted for the future. Hell, I've told him things that I've never told anyone, not even Morgan or Ma Brackenstone."

Ginger gave him a considering look. "This bothers you a lot, huh? We were never the kind of friends who confided in one another like this."

"Is it a problem?"

She smiled, eyes soft. "Of course not. It's just surprising. I remember you would always go to Morgan or Ma with your troubles."

"Morgan is busy with Wyatt and the kids, and I don't want to bother him." He laughed. "Ma has been stalking the Half Moon Guild Master. The man is Beck's mate, so her attention is focused on him."

Ginger snorted. "I miss that woman. I really should have called more."

"You went to Burnished Outpost, right?"

She nodded. "They needed pilot training."

"How'd it go?"

She arched a brow. "No changing the topic. Your captain is acting funny and it upsets you."

Lucas wiped his hands over his face. "Yeah. Let's remind me about that."

"Sounds like he caught the feels."

He gave her a confused look. "Huh?"

Ginger leaned forward, eyes bright. "You were friends for a while, and now he wants more. Think about it. He acts territorial over you and is suddenly self-conscious about how he looks when he's around you."

Lucas's eyes widened, and he felt his ears perk up. "He's demisexual."

She shrugged. "It took him some time to fall for you. Now he wants you and doesn't know how to deal with it."

A shadow fell over their table. "Lieutenant Meluth."

Lucas growled. Reed and Yeardley stood together. "What?"

Reed narrowed his eyes. "I had heard you were respectful."

"To those that deserve it," Lucas said, his curled lip

baring a fang. "When you get your head out of your ass and treat my captain better, then I'll consider showing you respect."

Reed looked like he'd swallowed a lemon, and Yeardley's face turned red.

"Hi," Ginger said brightly, kicking him under the table. "Pull up a chair if you'd like."

The two captains exchanged a reluctant look, then grabbed chairs.

Table's too small for this shit, Lucas thought. He had read Draif's reports on the three annoying captains earlier that day, but he still wanted to send all three out an airlock.

"We noticed your fighters were missing from training today," Yeardley said. "We just wanted to make sure you were keeping an eye on them. Anders is young, and Crimson and Ned are new recruits."

Lucas thought back to their intense training session with the assassins that morning. Draif had followed it up with a meditation hour, then target practice. Draif had checked in with the rest of the crew after lunch while Anders kept the other soldiers training.

"They're doing fine," he said, shaking his head. "You don't need to check in with us. The captain is good at his job."

Yeardley arched a brow. "Really? Then why do we seldom see him with the rest of the fleet captains? Does he have better things to do than talk strategy? Humans First will be coming for Charybdis Station. That's a fact."

Juniper interrupted them, setting Ginger and Lucas's plates in front of them.

The Fallon gave the two captains an annoyed look. "Are you two going on about Draif again? I told you yesterday. If you can't respect my friends, you don't get to enjoy my cooking."

Lucas watched them for a moment. "Instead of asking why my captain isn't training the crew as you would, maybe ask what he *is* doing. I'll tell you again – he's a good captain."

"He's a danger to your crew and to the station," Reed said angrily. "He should be a soldier on someone's ship, not a damn captain."

"Is your ass jealous of the shit coming out of your mouth?" Lucas asked dryly.

Yeardley and Reed stood, red-faced, and left the diner without another word.

Juniper huffed. "I don't understand them."

Ginger swallowed a bite of her sandwich. "Rumor is that those two and Wyther are convinced Draif Ando is incompetent. They're determined to prove he's unfit for the position."

Juniper rolled his eyes. "You know, all Draif would need to do is train his guys with the others or spend some time with those three."

Lucas started cutting his steak. "He barely has time to eat and sleep, little less go out for drinks at one of the bars. As for training, I think his sneaky brain *wants* them to underestimate him and our crew."

"What's he so busy with?" Ginger asked.

"He's determined to take on Humans First. We

know they'll come for the station, but Draif wants to whittle them down as much as possible before they get here."

Ginger's mouth dropped open.

Lucas grinned, pride filling him. "I told you he was a good captain. Draif is the most persistent over-achiever I've ever met. When he sets a goal, he doesn't stop until he accomplishes it. Humans First have caught his eye, and they'll regret it."

Ginger's eyes softened. "Oh, Lucas. You have it bad."

Juniper sighed. "He really does. Wait. Are you two on a date?"

Ginger choked on her food, hacking and wheezing until she was able to swallow. "No. We *are not* on a date."

Juniper gave him a curious look, and Lucas shrugged. "She thinks Draif will hunt her down if she tries anything with me."

She gulped down some water. "I did my research. He has connections, and I don't want to be on his bad side."

Juniper chuckled. "It's not his connections you need to worry about."

Lucas grinned. "I don't know. Leti and Princess Buttercup are fierce."

"Princess has a mean bite," Juniper agreed. "The thing is, Draif will make it last longer and hurt more."

3

Draif hurriedly surveyed his surroundings. Something stalked him.

Several months ago, Leti, Sebastian, and Draif had decided to combine their backyards so Wobble and Trixie would have more room to roam. The llama and goat had appreciated having more flowers to destroy.

Now, though, the backyard wasn't a place for leisure—it was a hunting ground.

He ducked behind a large chair in the backyard when he caught movement from the corner of his eye, then immediately slid across the ground to a flowering bush.

He peered through the thick branches and saw the Betonize Hunting cat scanning the open area. The cat was almost as big as Gravy, Hack's Old-Earth Newfoundland mix. The tip of one ear was missing, and his thick coat hid several scars.

Crouched at the cat's side was a young Betonize boy

with bright-green eyes, sharp fangs, and tiny claw-tipped hands.

Sami's face scrunched up in concentration as he looked around the yard. His hand rested in the thick fur on Pax's flank.

He pointed to the right, and Pax slid that way, feline body sleek and graceful. Sami headed left, frighteningly quiet for a kid who was barely four years old.

Draif moved backward, looking around for a larger hiding spot.

Unfortunately, Wobble was directly behind him, eating a flower from the bush Draif was hiding in.

Draif bumped him, and Wobble startled, letting out a weird, rhythmic bleating.

"Found you, Uncle Draif," Sami said, pouncing on his back.

Draif caught the boy's legs around his waist and held him steady. "I didn't know Wobble was on your side."

Sami reached out and patted the llama's head. "Wobble's on the flowers' side. You gots between him and his food."

Draif sighed. "Amateur mistake."

"Yep."

Pax sat on his haunches and watched them. Draif swore the cat's eyes laughed at him.

Sami leaned over his shoulder and pressed his cheek to Draif's. "Why you so sad?"

"How do you know I'm sad?"

Sami gave him a kiss. "Your eyes don't hide you."

Draif smiled. The kid was smart.

Leti came to the back door, Pepper balanced on his hip. He smiled at them. "You two ready for dinner?"

"We are," Draif said, happy to avoid Sami's question.

He knew why he was sad. Lucas had left him less than an hour ago to go eat dinner with that horrible woman. From his research, he knew Ginger Telbea was a top-notch pilot who had spent most of the past year on Burnished Outpost, training the Burnished to fly their antique ships. *Bitch.*

Leti frowned. "Why are you sad?"

"That's what I asked," Sami said, nodding at his dad.

"Is Hack in? I thought we might talk about some information I found."

Leti shook his head. "No. He's with Fasi and the Council. They're discussing the Bracken."

Just a day ago, Hack's best friend, Beck, had announced to the Council he and two others had created sentient androids. He was hoping the Council would acknowledge them as a species for their own protection.

Draif had never seen the Council so excited. The implications were endless, and they had a lot of tough decisions to make.

Leti let them into the kitchen. Rizzie already sat at the table next to the baby's high chair. Her feet swung back and forth as she waited patiently with a stuffed purple wolf in her lap.

Milo sat up in his high chair, watching them with bright golden-green eyes. His bronze skin was decorated with natural birthmarks that resembled sharp lined tattoos. Thick, wine-red hair covered his head.

He was the perfect blend of Hack and Leti.

Draif looked around the large kitchen. "Where's Mo and the others?"

Leti set Pepper in her highchair and peeled a giggling Sami from Draif's back. "Grandpa Moses took him, Alex, and Rose to the spaceport. They're meeting some friends from Burnished Outpost."

"How many came this time?"

"Almost twenty," Leti said with a grin. "They're going to focus on engineering and piloting for now. Then they'll see if any are better suited to other roles."

Since Burnished Outpost had gone through a shift in leadership, the planet was working closely with others in the system to learn all the skills needed to again be spacefaring.

"What about Maia, Wolf, and Silas?" Draif had gotten use to Leti's guards being a constant presence.

"Silas and Rune are having a private dinner at their place," Leti said, snickering.

"They're loving on each other," Rizzie said.

Draif grinned. *Yeah, I bet they are*, he thought.

"Maia and Wolf are patrolling the neighborhood. Haroon is guarding the house while they're gone. Last I checked, he was on the front porch," Leti said. "Sit."

Rizzie gave Draif a woeful look. "We're eating Daddy's cooking."

Draif winced. "Why didn't you come get me? I wouldn't have minded cooking."

Leti cleared his throat and glared at them. "We're

having salad with grilled chicken. That's it."

Rizzie slumped in relief. "Salad is easy."

"I can cook just fine," Leti said, scowling.

He brought a huge bowl of cut greens and vegetables and a plate of cooked and chopped chicken to the table.

Draif eyed the chicken, then used his fork to poke through it. "Alright. It looks completely cooked."

Leti huffed, then dished up their plates for them. "You two are worse than Will."

Draif smiled, then took a bite of the salad. It was edible.

Sami growled and used both hands to stuff chicken in his mouth, completely ignoring the vegetables.

Draif snuck a piece to Pax. The large cat stretched out under Sami's chair, catching any scraps the boy dropped.

Draif looked around again. "Where's Princess? He never misses dinner."

"He went with Fire," Rizzie said between bites. "They needed to take baby Stardust home."

Draif snickered. Leti's large Fire Veil Dragon had taken a liking to Morgan's baby Frost Veil Dragon. Almost every day, Princess went to Morgan's house to collect Stardust. After a day of playing, eating, and napping, the dragon escorted the baby home again.

"Frosty," Pepper called out, throwing her pudgy arms in the air.

Leti grinned. "She wants a dragon of her own."

Rizzie groaned. "Can't we get another bunny instead?"

"Daddy," Sami said, interrupting them. "Uncle Draif was sad."

Draif scowled. Damn kid really was smart.

Leti leaned over to kiss Sami's messy cheek. "You're right, baby boy. I almost forgot." He looked at Draif, green eyes narrowed. "What's wrong, Draif?"

"Nothing."

Rizzie eyed him. "Where's Uncle Lucas?"

Leti blinked. "Uh, where *is* Lucas? He's usually with you."

Draif scowled. "He's on a date."

"What?" Leti stood from the table, furious. "What do you mean he's on a date?"

Pepper frowned and banged the table. "No!"

Draif leaned back, feeling smug. They understood Lucas shouldn't be with the horrible woman too.

"He went to dinner with this woman he used to be friends with." Draif curled his lip. "She's atrocious. Her name is Ginger Telbea, and she's a pilot."

Leti eyed him suspiciously. "Why is she atrocious?"

"She has these stupid eyes that heat up when she looks at Lucas like he's a piece of meat. She hugged him, Leti. Hugged. Him."

Rizzie tilted her head and gave him a puzzled look.

"Ginger Telbea, you say?" Leti sat back down. "Hmm. Alex and Rose know her from her time on Burnished Outpost."

"Her eyes are stupid, Leti."

His friend nodded, face solemn. "I see."

"Xu and me can have a talk with her," Rizzie said. "Maybe she doesn't know Uncle Lucas is yours. This girl named Myrtle tried to take my stuffie at school, and Xu and me had to tell her to back off. We can do that for you, Uncle Draif."

Draif and Leti shared a wide-eyed look.

"Please let her do this, Leti."

"I'll be honest here. I really, really want to, but Will may object if we use Rizzie as a gang enforcer."

Rizzie leaned forward, arm braced on the table. "You gotta be tough with people, Uncle Draif. She must not know Uncle Lucas is yours. We need to tell her."

Leti put more chicken onto Sami's plate before he went back to feeding Milo. "Is Lucas yours, Draif?"

Draif swallowed hard. "He's my friend."

Rizzie shook her head. "Nuh-uh. You love him. Like my daddies love each other. Like Uncle Silas and Uncle Rune love each other too. Best friends don't feel that way. Xu and me are best friends, so I know how it is."

Leti looked at Rizzie like she'd grown another head. "When did you figure out love, ladybug?"

She shrugged. "You and Daddy Will look at each other like Uncle Lucas looks at Uncle Draif. I'm not stupid. That means it's love."

Leti reached out and took his hand. "Is it love, Draif?"

Draif shook his head. "It can't be. It would mess everything up."

Rizzie looked confused. "How?"

"Yes, Draif," Leti said. "How?"

"Just because I care about him *that way*, doesn't mean he cares about me like that."

"Didn't you just hear me," Rizzie said, disgruntled.

"He loves you. I see it all the time."

Leti grinned. "Listen to Rizzie, Draif. My girl knows what she's talking about."

Draif shook his head. Rizzie was just a couple of years older than Sami. She couldn't possibly tell the difference between friendship and love.

After dinner, they moved to the living room. Rizzie settled with Sami in front of the vid-screen to watch cartoons, and Pax stretched out beside Sami. Princess made it back home and lay on a cushioned bed under the front window. The dragon looked exhausted from dealing with baby Stardust all day.

Even Leti's Druffle were visiting tonight. The strange little balls of fluff ran back and forth through the tunnels that lined most of the rooms in the house. Leti's original nest had tripled in size since they moved to Charybdis Station, so Pops had designed more tunnels and hutches for them throughout the house.

Leti leaned into Draif, arms wrapping around him. "You love Lucas. Don't you?"

Draif settled his head on his friend's shoulder. "I don't want to be stupid again."

"Lucas isn't like Beldon Cortez."

"I know," Draif said. "He's a wonderful man who doesn't deserve to have to put up with a mess like me."

Leti glared at him, real anger in his eyes. "Don't you dare say things like that, Draif. You're as close to perfect as any person can possibly be."

Draif laughed, face buried against Leti's stupid llama sweater. "I love you, Leti. You're a delusional weirdo, but I love you."

4

Later that evening, Draif sat beside Ava in the Lord Admiral's office.

Fasi Juren was a large purple Grell with a kind disposition but a wicked sense of justice. The Lord Admiral wanted to protect the people of his station, and he was a fighter. He wouldn't stand back when he could help those in need.

He had Draif's complete respect and his utter loyalty.

Right now, his broad, furry face was both solemn and determined. "You two have a report for me on HF?"

Draif closed his eyes and breathed deeply before answering. "It's bad. I found quite a bit of information on their leadership and infrastructure while Ava focused on their strategy with the rest of the galaxy."

Hack spoke up from his seat near the window. "We've seen the public list of members, but who are these people?"

"Publicly, they are a coalition of like-minded businesspeople that are promoting human superiority," Draif said.

Ava pulled up several lists and charts on her tablet, projecting the images for them to see. "They are trying to convince the public that the human species is more intelligent and better equipped to rule the galaxy. Here is a list of companies that were *encouraged* to hire a human CEO."

Fasi frowned. "How were they encouraged?"

Ava scowled. "Each company's previous CEO was either a victim of one of Air's attacks or has mysteriously disappeared."

"Fuckers," Hack muttered.

Ava pointed at another list. "These are industry leaders that rejected trade or shipping agreements for the public members of HF. They have each conveniently died and been replaced with a human sympathetic to HF."

"You keep saying *public* members," Fasi said.

Draif cleared his throat. "There are more people on HF's side than appear on their manifesto. They have connections everywhere and not all of them are human."

"Who the fuck are they?" Hack asked angrily. "There are not a lot of pure-blooded humans in the galaxy, if any. Why the hell do people support them?"

"Money," Draif said simply. "These people are disgustingly wealthy. They've inherited fortunes and businesses and have only continued to flourish and grow."

He projected the images of four faces from his tablet. "HF is controlled by three men and one woman. Harrison Goel owned the medical research and development institution that ran Dr. Morrick's lab. His focus has been in pharmaceuticals and medical research."

Fasi considered the man's picture. "He knew about the artifact?"

Draif pulled up a copy of a message sent between Goel's personal assistant and the lab supervisor. "One of my contacts dug this up and sent it to me. Goel is the one who arranged for the artifact to *find* itself in Dr. Morrick's hands."

Samson, G wants you to keep the package secure as Dr. Morrick works on it. Our associates weren't happy it disappeared, but G wants leverage. He wants complete control of the Element. No matter what, do not let it leave Frost Veil. Sharp will be your contact. Keep G's name out of it for now.

"Okay," Hack said, rubbing his chin. "Goel arranged for Death's artifact to be sent to Morrick so that he could keep control of the situation."

"Most likely, control of the Queen," Draif said, shrugging.

Fasi's smile was a little too predatory. "That backfired."

"Yeah," Draif said, thinking of their friend Death. The being cohabited Dr. Morrick's body and had made an excellent ally.

"It's also important to note that he is a direct competitor with our own medical research division,"

Ava said, face concerned. "For the last ten years, Dr. Orsla and the other scientists have made major contributions to the pharmaceutical industry. We've gained his attention."

"What about the others you mentioned?" Hack asked.

"Goel definitely leads them, both privately and publicly, but the other three aren't exactly lightweights," Draif said. "Goel's closest friend, Sofus Hald, is an industrial giant in the medical field. He owns several factories on six different planets that are devoted solely to the production of medical equipment and pharmaceuticals. The man is one of the richest people in the galaxy. Goel and he work together often."

Fasi growled. "I met the asshole last year. He tried to strong-arm Charybdis when we were taking bids to produce and distribute Orsla's latest vaccine."

"He's not fond of Charybdis Station," Draif said, pulling up a new message.

G, when will we focus on CS? That fucking Grell bastard is using some Dedril on Beton to produce the Tesno vaccine. He made me a laughingstock, and I want that pathetic little station to burn.

"Well, that's not very nice," Hack said dryly.

"Here's Goel's response," Draif said.

Be patient. We have bigger concerns then a tiny backwater station.

Fasi grumbled. "Backwater? Charybdis Station is the greatest place in the galaxy!"

"Calm down, big guy," Ava said, laughter in her voice. "It's a good thing they underestimate us."

Draif hid his smile and continued. "We also have Teresa Malone, who basically owns most of Rueal in the Sugarworm System. She runs a large portion of the luxury goods market and, by my estimations, is the wealthiest of all of them." He sighed and pulled up another message. "She is also the one who gave the go ahead for the Concords to take Tammol. Apparently, Sharp approached her with the plan before attacking the planet."

Sharp, my darling. I would be quite happy to have the Concords as my neighbor in place of the wretched Tammolians. You have the unspoken support of Rueal, but remember, G wants this kept under the radar. Our time to go public hasn't come yet. If you have any survivors, remember I'm branching into the slave industry. Kisses! – T

"Kisses?" Hack looked disgusted. "Sharp and the Concords almost wiped out the Tammolian people, and she's asking for survivors to sell into slavery?"

Fasi's face was grim. "Who is the last one?"

Draif was quiet for a minute. "Nelson Cortez. He is another industrial giant, but focuses on tech production. He owns his own small industrial world and lives on Vextonar. His estate is actually next-door to Goel's."

"What aren't you saying?" Fasi said, eyes narrowed.

Draif looked away. "It's nothing important nor related."

"Draif." Fasi's tone was firm. "Tell us."

"Cortez's eldest son is Beldon Cortez. We have history."

Ava leaned over and tipped his face toward hers,

stroking the scars on his cheeks. "Is he the one that did this?"

Draif shook his head. "No. Well, not directly."

Fasi stood and knelt next to his chair. "Explain, Draif."

Draif sighed. "It's not important."

"Leave him alone," Hack said. "He's allowed his secrets."

Draif's laugh was hollow, even to his ears. "It's not a secret. Leti and Lucas both know."

"Please, Draif," Fasi asked. "You've never spoken of your parents or your life before Leti."

He didn't want Fasi's pity. He wanted his respect.

The Lord Admiral's big eyes pleaded with him. *Damn it!*

"I was born into slavery on Vextonar," Draif said. "My father was a Lower. He was a Wello-Human hybrid. My mother was a full-blooded Wello and a wealthy businessman's bed-slave. He wasn't too happy when she got pregnant, especially not when he found out it was by another man."

"What did your father do?" Fasi asked.

"He couldn't afford to buy her or me, not that our owner would have sold us. Cook told me he disappeared soon after I was born."

"What about your mother?" Hack asked.

Draif shrugged. "She died when I was almost two."

Ava put her hand on his shoulder and squeezed.

"I remember some things," Draif said, smiling softly. "I remember her hugging me and singing. Her hugs were like Leti's – soft and loving." He shook his head.

"It wasn't too bad at first. I ran errands for my owner and got to go to the spaceport a lot. I met Dottie there."

Hack grinned. "I bet she loved you."

Draif smiled crookedly. "Yeah. She always fed me and told me stories about all the other worlds she had visited." His smile faded. "When I was thirteen, it was decided I was pretty enough to be a bed-slave, so they sold me to the local training compound."

Fasi's hand gripped the arm of the chair. "You were a child!"

"I wasn't exactly cooperative," Draif said, smiling wryly. "I had a habit of attacking my trainers."

"Good," Fasi said through gritted teeth.

"When I was fifteen, I met Beldon. He was a few years older and was handsome and kind. I met him at the compound, but he said he hated slavery and was trying to find a way to free everyone there. He came back, day after day, and took the time to talk to me."

Ava reached out and took his hand.

"I fell for him. Completely. He became my world, and I was so sure we had a future together," Draif said, voice soft. "He told me he loved me, and I believed him. I let myself trust him. For two months, we would meet at night and fuck."

Draif closed his eyes, remembering how he had felt loved and cherished. He had been so eager for more than just the sex. He had *needed* to be held. To feel as if he had value.

"Gods damn it, Draif." Fasi's voice was even and hard. The arm of the chair cracked in the large man's grip.

"That last night, he brought the owner of the training compound with him. They were friends. Beldon told him I was a good fuck and to send me back to him once I was finished training."

"That bastard," Hack said, eyes filling with his inner fire. The tattoos along his arms beginning to light up as well.

Draif flushed. "I was so stupid. I thought it was his way of getting me out of there. Then I met the others. Beldon had a habit of fucking around with the new trainees. He paid the compound owner a monthly fee, and when he found one he liked well enough, he bought him. It was his way of sampling the wares."

Draif swallowed. He had been devastated. Nothing had mattered anymore, and he had wanted to die. He had wanted the pain to be over.

He laughed bitterly. "His friend had even made a wager with him. He *dared* Beldon to break me in. Said no one could do it."

"I'll kill him," Fasi said, teeth gritted. "I'll kill the bastard."

Hack tilted his head, eyes full of golden flames. "Just need to be near him to burn a fucking hole through him."

Ava's voice was like a sudden ice bath. "Explain your scars, darling. Had they not hurt you enough?"

Draif shrugged. "I didn't take Beldon's betrayal well and killed a couple of trainers. The compound owner decided I was too broken to be useful, so he wanted to kill me. Someone recommended maiming instead. They said it would break my spirit, and I could still be sold as a work-slave." He touched his scars. "Leti's dad happened to stop by after it was done. I was in bad shape, so he bought me and gave me to Leti. Told him to *dominate the broken bed-slave like a real man.*"

Ava's brow raised. "We see how well that worked."

Draif smiled. "I wasn't nice. I tried to attack Leti, but I was too weak. He took care of me. Had Princess Buttercup sleep beside me while I healed. He kept bringing his pets to visit with me as he read me stories. He loved me, *really loved me,* and I've been his ever since."

Hack's eyes slowly dimmed to his normal hue. "I take it neither Leti nor Lucas know about Cortez's involvement."

Draif shrugged. "I haven't mentioned it."

Leti wouldn't be happy when he found out.

"We'll kill Cortez, Draif," Fasi said. "I promise you, we will kill the bastard."

Draif nodded, then straightened in his seat. "Beldon is hip deep in HF, so yes, we will. Now, back to Humans First. The four lead a coalition of people just like them. They are savage and will let no one stand in their way, human or not. Their strength is in their wealth and connections. That buys soldiers and ships, bribes non-humans to support them, and gives them access to a lot of resources that we simply don't have."

Ava nodded. "It truly is dire. Both Vextonar and Rueal are very sympathetic to HF. Vextonar is one of the largest shipping hubs in the galaxy, and Rueal is the second largest. Humans First has the manpower and industry resources to control the galaxy."

"They also have the Queen and Earth," Hack said. "They can destroy a world in one day."

"Speaking of that," Draif said, "Ava and I found an interesting pattern."

"One we already suspected," Ava said, eyes sad. "We understand why Water and the Concords attacked Tammol, but the others seemed random, though we suspected their destruction somehow benefitted HF."

"Bredell was Air's first known victim," Draif said. "Hald and Malone had major competitors vacationing on the resort planet when it was destroyed. They were all killed along with their immediate families."

"Dairilve was another of Air's victims," Ava said. "Two of Cortez's rivals were vacationing there when it was destroyed. Both Malone and Cortez quickly picked up their clients. Somehow, Malone even managed to claim one of the men's estate and businesses."

"Icewilde was another victim of Air," Draif said. "It was a major industrial world. Cortez and Hald joined together and are in negotiations to buy up the land and rebuild."

"Then there is Union Station," Ava said. "The planet had a poor relationship with Vextonar and refused to deal with any one planet. They were open to all. Now, Vextonar has a spaceport built atop the rubble."

Hack rubbed his face. "What about Elusa?"

"It was full of activists and wealthy non-human celebrities." Draif brought an image up. "This was Danellia Sola. She was a Drellian celebrity who was very outspoken about her support of diversity and tolerance. She specifically spoke out against Goel's specieism and aggressive business policies."

"She wasn't the only one to die there," Ava said. "The loss of so many beloved and well-known individuals has had an impact on the galaxy's morale."

"These are our enemies," Fasi said, returning to his seat.

"Yes," Draif said. "I've compiled detailed reports and sent them to both of you. There's something Ava and I don't understand though."

"Their businesses rely on consumers," Ava said. "While pure-blooded humans are rare, human hybrids are plentiful. However, they by no means dominate the galaxy's population. HF's leadership has lost business because of this. As much as they reduce their competition, they lose customers to much smaller businesses because of their association with the Queen."

"It's as if they're sabotaging themselves, and I don't understand it," Draif said.

"The impact their tactics are having on the galaxy is disturbing as well," Ava said. "So many are starting to panic and back away from working with any other species. Dramacus and Siletus have both recently passed policies to exile all non-native species. I've included details in my report, but this is truly alarming."

"The galactic economy relies on trade agreements and cooperation," Draif said. "This is just bad business."

Fasi looked between them. "Do you two have any

suggestions before I bring this to the Council and start strategizing?"

Draif smiled. "Their power comes from the Queen and from their wealth. I can't offer you any insight into the Queen, but I have some plans that I've already put into place to, uh, decrease their wealth. They're losing business with their choice of tactics, but they're still turning a profit. Give me the go ahead, and I'll do my best to change that."

Fasi looked at him a moment. "Will you make yourself a target?"

"No more than Charybdis Station already is. They will come for us. There's no doubt of that. The weaker they are when they get here, the better."

Fasi nodded. "Do it."

"While he focuses on weakening HF's foundation, you and I need to start recruiting more allies," Ava said. "We've created bonds with the other planets in our system, but I would like to solidify them. HF won't fall easily, and they threaten more than Charybdis Station and more than the Anchors Rest System."

"I'm all for more allies," Fasi said, nodding. "I'll let the diplomatic division know you're heading this and to give you support. What do you need from me?"

"I need you and your charming nature, not the diplomatic division," she said, then gave him a hard look. "We're not negotiating an agreement or policy change. It's time to cut through the bullshit and get the job done. The galaxy is on the brink of complete chaos. Now isn't the time to kiss ass and discuss import and export fees. We've collected many mercenary groups to work with us against the Queen. Now I want to use those connections to plan our attack. I need you with me in each discussion."

Hack's eyes widened. "What are you planning?"

"We can't take HF down alone, nor should we." Ava leaned forward. "It's time the galaxy worked together."

5

The next morning, Lucas watched Draif nervously as he talked with Olla in the commons of their ship. Their pilot was working through a new set of flight simulations alongside Draif and wanted to talk strategy.

Tae, their engineer, came to stand beside him. "What did you do?"

Lucas eyed the gruff, dark-skinned man. "Huh?"

"Captain's mad."

Lucas's tail swished back and forth behind him. "I don't know. He didn't eat his breakfast this morning and would barely talk to me."

Lucas thought back to that morning. Draif hadn't even bothered to look at him, and Princess Buttercup had watched them through the kitchen window, hissing. Lucas thought the dragon might be planning on eating him.

Brenna looked up from where she sat reading her tablet. "You went on a date."

Tae frowned. "What the fuck, Lucas?"

Lucas rolled his eyes. "It wasn't a date. Even if it was though, it wouldn't matter."

"The hell it wouldn't," Tae said. "You belong to the Captain."

Lucas's ears shot up, and he tilted his head. "Say what?"

"Lucas," Brenna said, giving him a pitying look. "We all know you're in love with him."

Lucas groaned. "I really didn't need to know everyone thinks I'm pathetic."

"You're not pathetic." Tae smacked his back. "The last few months, the Captain's been watching you differently."

"That's what Ginger said." Lucas frowned. "Do you really think he wants me now?"

"You're life mates, so of course he does," Brenna said. The Siren yawned before going back to her reading.

The clawed tips of Lucas's fingers cut into the palm of his hand as he clenched his fist. "How do you know that?"

Brenna looked up and winced. "Okay, so Nettle may have told me. He wanted me to keep an eye on you since you've been pining over the Captain for so long."

Tae chuckled. "He almost swooned yesterday when the Captain thanked him for working with Ned on his target practice."

"I don't *swoon*," Lucas growled.

Tae snickered. "Your eyes do get big and moony."

"Anyway," Brenna said, rolling her eyes. "Maybe you need to explain your *date* wasn't a date."

"What date?" Draif asked. Lucas almost jumped. Draif was a quiet fucker when he wanted to be.

Lucas cleared his throat. "Just so you know. I wasn't on a date last night. I met Ginger at Juniper's, and we had dinner. Then she went her way and I went home. Where, I might add, you weren't at."

"I had a meeting with Fasi, Ava, and Hack," Draif said, a slow smile spreading across his face. "Not a date, huh?"

"Nope."

"I looked her up." Draif shrugged, a smile tugging at his lips. "She's a good pilot and loyal to the station. That doesn't mean she's good enough for you though."

Lucas grinned. "She looked you up too."

Draif's brows rose. "Don't make me like the woman, Lucas. That's going too far."

Brenna's dark eyes glittered with amusement, and she tapped a finger against one dark purple cheek. "I think you and Ginger would make good friends, Captain. You both are insanely talented, like being prepared, and for some reason think Lucas is an alright kind of guy."

Lucas gave her a dry look. "Thanks, Brenna. You're so kind."

Draif looked around. "What are you all standing around for? Tae, did you finish installing the newest shielding tech? Brenna, what about the med bay inventory?"

"On it, Captain," Tae said, not bothering to hide his smile as he ran from the room.

Brenna grinned. "I finished the inventory yesterday. We're good."

Lucas's comm buzzed, and he answered the call. "Finn?"

"We have a problem," Finn said, voice grim. "A group of assassins infiltrated the station and attempted to kidnap one of the Bracken in Half Moon territory."

Lucas closed his eyes. Sadly, this didn't surprise him. The technology behind the Bracken far surpassed anything the galaxy had ever seen.

"They need us?" Draif asked, pulling Lucas's arm towards him.

"We're good now," Finn said. "Though another medic would be appreciated."

"I'm on my way," Brenna said from over Draif's shoulder. "Be there in ten."

"We need to keep this as private as possible," Finn said. "I've reviewed footage and found where they came in, but they had the appropriate paperwork."

Lucas frowned. "That means someone signed off on it. Let me ask a few questions and call you back."

"Thanks," Finn said. "I'm working with Enforcement to make sure no others have slipped through."

"I'm going to check on Leti," Draif said, biting his lip. "I just need to make sure he's okay. The Concords are gone, but he's still a target as long as the Queen is out there."

Lucas nodded and watched Draif run from the ship. Charybdis Station was supposed to be a safe haven.

"I'll message you what I find out," Lucas told Finn, then ended the call.

He quickly connected another vid-call with his friend at the docks. It would be quicker to go around the proper channels.

"Hey, Lucas." Renni's narrow face lit up. "I saw Ginger last night, and she told me some interesting news about you."

Lucas smirked. "I bet she did. Tell me later. The Lord Admiral needs information, fast."

———

LATER THAT EVENING, LUCAS SAT IN THE WINDOW SEAT of Draif's office, Marmalade in his lap. His friend Morgan sat beside him, his small Frost Veil Dragon stretched across his shoulders. Ava paced back and forth in front of them while Draif stood at his desk, looking at the various screens projected in the air around him.

"Brinanda," Draif said thoughtfully. He tapped and spun a screen around, reviewing the information, thumb pressed against his bottom lip.

"I hate this," Ava said, golden face troubled. "She's Fallon and had a good relationship with the Prime Minister on Fallow. This is a diplomatic nightmare."

"Beck and the Council didn't take it well," Morgan said. "Poor Beck."

"One of our own Council members betrayed us," Lucas said, voice low. "I can't see anyone taking it well."

They had quickly discovered that Councilwoman Brinanda was the one that organized the attempted abduction of one of the Bracken with the hope of selling him to the highest bidder.

"Malone," Draif said, voice hard. "Brinanda tried to sell the information to a company on Rueal affiliated with Malone. The owner is a member of Humans First."

"I can't see Brinanda joining HF," Morgan said.

"No," Draif agreed. "She didn't contact the company."

Lucas exchanged looks with Morgan.

Draif turned around and held his tablet up, showing them the message there. "Look. Someone contacted her almost immediately after the Council meeting. HF has someone watching us. Probably someone within Fasi's office."

Councilwoman – Charybdis Station will fall. Humans First cannot be defeated; however, we are not unsympathetic to you and the Fallon. You understand credits run this galaxy. Peridot Technologies will pay well for any information you have on the Bracken. We are also prepared to offer you the use of our colleagues to obtain one of the specimens.

Draif turned back around and tapped another screen. "Peridot Tech has contracted the Equinox Assassins Guild several times in the past. For this to happen so quickly, HF's contact here on the station must be someone close and someone easily overlooked.

The Lord Admiral has three personal assistants. I'll start looking into them."

"Lucas and I will go have a talk with Fasi," Morgan said. "We'll do it in person."

Draif grabbed Lucas's arm, fingers gentle and warm. "Keep your eyes open and be careful."

Lucas smiled and patted his friend's hand. "I will."

Ava and Morgan stared at Draif's hand on Lucas's arm for a long moment.

Draif cleared his throat, cheeks flushed. "Thank you."

Lucas and Morgan hurried down the stairs. They met Fire at the door. The Element looked sleepy and grumpy.

"Fire?" Lucas raised his brow. "Can I help you?"

"I need a nap."

"Okay?"

"Marmalade takes the best naps." Fire pushed passed him and ran up the stairs.

Lucas exchanged a look with Morgan, then shrugged. "Apparently, Fire likes to take naps with our cat."

"He comes by the house to play with Luna and Stardust too," Morgan said.

Lucas laughed.

"So," Morgan said as they walked toward the tram. "Am I the only one who noticed that look in Draif's eyes?"

Lucas shrugged and tried to shove down the hope bubbling up. He had waited so long for Draif to take notice of him.

"Lucas?"

He pulled his friend on the tram, then looked around before leaning close. "You aren't the only one noticing, and I think you're right. It's finally time."

Morgan whooped loudly and hugged him. "Finally. You two are practically married already."

"Keep it down," Lucas said, shushing his friend. "I haven't talked to him yet. I'll get to it once things calm down around here."

Morgan didn't stop grinning.

"You look stupid," Lucas said, grumbling.

"You're going to be mated, then the babies will come, and then you'll be a cranky old man yelling at a giant Fire Veil Dragon to get off your lawn."

Lucas raised a brow. "Princess is more than welcome on our lawn." *Well, as long as he doesn't want to eat me*, he thought.

Morgan stroked Stardust's head. "Wait until he steals your precious little pet every day. Then tell me Princess is welcome."

They were almost to the governmental buildings when Yeardley, Wyther, and Reed found them.

Lucas groaned. "What the fuck do you three want now?"

Reed arched a brow. "What are you doing here? Shouldn't you be training with your crew?"

Morgan looked between them. "Why the fuck are you questioning Lucas? His weapons specialist is working with the crew, just like most of yours are."

"Is Anders really equipped for that?" Wyther asked, frowning.

Lucas gave Morgan a look. "I told you they were like this, didn't I?"

Morgan shook his head, eyes full of disbelief. "I thought you were exaggerating. Damn."

Lucas cleared his throat. "We have business to take care of."

"Is it the Bracken?" Yeardley asked, eyes brightening. "Do you need help with them? The story of Engineer Brackenstone's creations is all over the station."

Lucas thought Beck's Bracken and the Charybdis Fyrlings were probably going to be the topic of choice for a while.

Lucas considered them. "Okay. Here's the deal. This constant questioning shit can't go on. Draif is convinced you three will calm down with time, but it's damned annoying having to defend my actions every time I'm in public."

Reed's eyes narrowed. "What are you implying?"

"I'm not implying," Lucas said. "I'm saying, you three need to back off. However, I've read your dossiers, and I know you won't unless you feel like my captain can be trusted."

"Our dossiers?" Wyther looked furious.

Morgan grinned. "Draif researched them, didn't he?"

"Of course he did." Lucas glared at the three captains. "Now, keep an eye on your comms. Draif will pull you three into his web soon enough. He wouldn't have put up with your shit for so long if he didn't think you were worth trusting."

He pushed around the captains and strode toward the building. He didn't relish having to tell Fasi they had a mole, but it was still better than dealing with those three.

———

A few days later, Fasi, Renee, and the entirety of the Council sat in Hack and Leti's living room.

Fasi bounced Pepper on his knee, eyes sad. "I can't believe Harley, Fergus, or Kaylessa would betray us."

"I don't think many thought Brinanda would," Leti said scowling. "Imprisonment is too good for her."

"Your assistants are only three of the suspects," Draif said. "It may not be them, but they're closest to you.

Lucas wrinkled his nose. Draif looked calm and collected, but Lucas knew his mate really liked Fasi's three assistants. It would upset him if one of them was the mole.

"Until we know for sure," Councilman Delino said, "we should have our more private discussions here."

Lucas looked around the crowded kitchen. "Our house is also open to you. Draif scans it for listening devices everyday already."

Leti snickered. "He does my house too."

Councilwoman Rundel raised a brow. "A little paranoid, are you?"

Draif shrugged. "The Concords kept sending assassins to kill Leti, and we have a lot of important conversations here. It seemed wise."

"Speaking of important conversations," Fasi said, eyes on Hack. "Son, are you sure you're alright to lead the fleet against the Queen?"

Lucas fought to keep his expression clear of his worry.

Earlier that day, the Council and Fasi had settled on a plan. Draif and Ava would lead the fight against Humans First here at the station, and Hack and a small fleet would go to fight the Queen and Earth in the Crellic System.

Lucas dreaded saying goodbye to his friends and knew Draif and Leti wouldn't take it well.

"I'm glad to do it," Hack said. "I don't relish being away from home, but I want this finished."

"Draif," Councilwoman Jalina said, "I know it's only been a few days since you spoke with the Lord Admiral, but have you made any progress against HF?"

Draif nodded. "I've started making contact with the big four's most recent victims and their current business competitors. Mostly, they're all frightened and trying to stay out of HF's way. However, there are two men in particular that want to help."

Councilman Delino looked skeptical. "Can they really be helpful? Won't that draw HF's attention directly to them?"

Draif's eyes lit up, and Lucas knew he was plotting something.

"I have a plan that should keep them under the radar. Well, at least until it's too late for HF," Draif said. "With your permission, I need to make a quick trip to Derelict to meet with both of them. The Blue Raven is fast, so it shouldn't take more than a week. I can give you more details then."

Fasi nodded. "Permission granted."

"Tomorrow morning, you, Renee, and I have an unofficial appointment with the Betonize president, three mercenary admirals, and the King of Grellweir," Ava said, patting Fasi's shoulder. "Please invite Sheiria; I'd like her input."

The Council members all stared at Ava in shock.

"What in the galaxy are you planning?" Councilman Warren asked, eyes wide.

Ava smiled serenely. "Just a little chat about Humans First. Nothing to worry about."

Draif's hand on Lucas's back distracted him. "Make sure you talk to Beck about those boots before they go. I can't wait to try them out."

Lucas nodded. Both he and Draif wanted a pair of the new altered gravitational hover boots Beck had designed. "You got it."

As the talk continued, the warm weight of Draif's hand stayed on his back, and Lucas couldn't help but hope it really was time.

The next day, Draif walked beside Leti as they headed toward one of the salons in the Blue Sector. Sami's little clawed hand was in his, and he kept a tight hold. The little boy was curious and liked to wander.

Pax paced beside them, trying to herd them away from the busy people they shared the walkway with.

Leti's guards, Maia and Silas, walked behind them with Rizzie between them. Their eyes scoured the crowd for any hint of danger.

"You can't go with them, Leti," Draif said, fear making his gut churn. "It's too dangerous, and I've already made a commitment to stay here."

After Fasi had announced to the rest of their group that Hack was leading a fleet to the Crellic System, Leti had surprised them all by declaring that he was also going.

Draif was handling it worse than Hack. He'd been badgering Leti about it since he found out.

Leti huffed and shifted Pepper to his other hip. "I have to go. I may just be a historian, but I have valuable insight into the Queen and her Elements."

"I don't want you to go," Draif said, eyes watering. "I can't be without you. You're my family."

Leti stopped in the middle of the busy walkway and pulled Draif into a hug.

Draif buried his face against Leti's soft shoulder and breathed in his scent.

Princess Buttercup didn't protest having to share Leti's shoulder. The dragon was in his traveling size and draped along Leti's shoulders. He rubbed his scaly head against Draif's.

Draif had never been apart from Leti since he was given to him, injured and broken. His head knew Leti was right. He really needed to go. Draif's heart just couldn't stand it.

"No matter what happens, I will always be with you," Leti whispered softly. "Your family is much bigger than you think, Draify. Ma and Renee have already agreed to keep an eye on you and Lucas for me. You're not alone anymore."

"I love you, Leti," Draif said, wiping his eyes on his friend's sweater. This one was covered in kittens.

"I need you to promise to be there for my kids," Leti said. "They understand what's happening, but the longer we're gone, the harder it will get."

"I'll guard them with my life. I swear."

"I know you will," Leti said, cupping his cheek. "I mean guard their hearts. Be there for them. Please?"

"Of course."

Sami squeezed Draif's hand. "We'll be 'kay, Uncle Draify. Daddy will come backs soon."

Draif let go of Leti and swung Sami up on his back. "You're right. Leti will be back before we know it. Let's go get your hair cut."

Sami scowled. "I don't wanna."

"Uncle Draify will get his cut too," Leti said, smiling. "I have pretty gold beads for both of you to put in your hair."

Draif glared at Leti. "My hair's fine."

"Mine too," Sami said, pouting.

Leti narrowed his eyes. "You two better not sass me. It's time for everyone to get their hair cut, and that's that. Will is even taking Mo, Alex, and Rose later today."

"Do Maia and Silas have to?" Draif waved at the guards behind them.

"Yes," Leti said, nodding firmly. "Everyone does. Now come on."

Draif and the others groaned but followed him.

His long dark hair was usually pulled back. When he left it down, it made a nice screen to hide his scars behind. Ginger's hair had been well-kept and stylish, Draif remembered. Maybe it wouldn't be so bad to get a new look.

It was unbearable. Sami insisted on sitting in his lap the whole time, and Leti kept calling out suggestions.

The stylist arched a brow. "I'm going to ignore the man in the horrible sweater, alright?"

Draif nodded. "Yeah, just make it nice, okay?"

The woman smiled softly. "Do you have someone to impress?"

"Uncle Lucas," Sami answered for him. "Fucking Ginger's trying to steal him."

Draif winced. He really needed to watch his language.

"Oh," the woman said, eyes lighting up. "I see how it is. Sit back, sweetheart. I'll take care of you."

An hour later, Draif stared in the mirror. His long hair was gone and a much shorter, spiky style was in its place. Gold beads were threaded through the short strands and contrasted well with his brown skin.

He felt oddly vulnerable. He wouldn't be able to hide his face anymore. The stylist seemed to read his mind as he touched his scars.

"Never hide that beautiful face of yours," she said, voice hard. "However those scars got there, they're a part of you. If this Lucas can't take that, then you come back to me. I'll treat you right."

Draif watched the dark cheeks of his reflection flush.

"Come on, Uncle Draify," Sami said, tapping him on the shoulder. "Pepper and Daddy are done too."

Draif thanked the woman and gave her a hefty tip before sitting beside Leti.

"You're so handsome," Leti said, patting his cheek.

"Me too, Daddy?" Sami looked up, his own haircut similar to Draif's.

Leti laughed and kissed his son's cheek. "You too, baby boy. Now we wait on Rizzie, Maia, and Silas, then we'll go home for a snack."

Sami yawned and snuggled against Draif's chest. "Okay." Pax settled at Draif's feet, bright eyes checking in on Sami.

Draif's comm buzzed, and he answered it. "Hey, Olla."

His pilot looked conflicted. "Can I meet with you, sir?"

Draif nodded, concerned. "Sure. Meet me at the house in about an hour."

"Thank you, Captain," she said and hurriedly ended the call.

Draif exchanged a look with Leti. "That was weird."

"What did you talk to Bendix about yesterday?" Leti asked. "I noticed you and him alone in the corner."

"Just an idea I had," Draif said, looking around the salon. He didn't think anyone was listening in on them but didn't want to risk it.

Draif hadn't liked the fact that the Equinox Guild had gotten into Charybdis Station as easily as they had. His research into the big four of HF's business tactics had worried him.

Bendix had agreed to work with Enforcement to make the station more secure and to keep two members of Half Moon on protection detail for the Lord Admiral until HF was taken care of. The station needed the Lord Admiral, and so did Leti and the others.

"Draif, I need you to promise me one more thing."

"Sure."

"I want you to tell Lucas how you feel. After we

leave in the morning, talk to him. Let him know you've fallen in love with him."

Draif clenched his fists, trying to hide their trembling. "I don't know, Leti."

"Please?" Leti's green eyes grew big and shiny. His bottom lip trembled.

"Damn it, Leti! Not the eyes."

"Please, Draif. For me?"

Draif groaned. "Alright. I promise."

Leti grinned. "Perfect!"

Draif glared at him and then changed the subject. "I meant to tell you, I have a call scheduled with Dottie tonight. I'll ask her about your friend Advaith. Okay?"

Leti blew Rizzie a kiss as she waved at him from her seat. "Thank you. I'm worried about him and his family. He said everything happened so quickly. One moment it was business as usual, then the next, the university was handing out the human-centric curriculum and canceling any research grants that weren't focused on Old-Earth. It's frightening how quickly things can go so badly."

"I can't imagine," Draif said, shaking his head. "With HF destroying so many planets, so easily, it has to be frightening. If the Queen is killed, then at least they'll have to work a hell of a lot harder to take out a planet."

"I hope you all make them bleed credits," Leti said. "That's all they care about, and I want them to lose everything. Just like the people they've killed."

Draif smiled. "They will. I promise."

———

DRAIF WAITED UNTIL LETI AND THE OTHERS WERE IN THE house before turning to his own.

Olla waited on his doorstep, looking close to tears.

Draif jogged to the door and unlocked it. "Come inside and tell me what's wrong."

The house seemed empty without Lucas in it. Draif's lieutenant was training with the others at Half Moon's training compound.

He led Olla to the couch and sat with her. "What's going on?"

Olla blew a strand of brown hair from her face. "I'm human."

Draif arched a brow. "Okay?"

She groaned. "This thing with Humans First is killing me. They say they represent *my* species, but they've killed billions of people. I can't take it."

"Olla, most people understand that Humans First don't speak for all humans. We don't think you're like them."

"I know. No one I've talked to thinks I'm like them, but it hurts me that they're doing this. I feel responsible somehow."

"You are not responsible for Humans First," Draif said sternly. "You have a good heart. I've seen how you are with others. You aren't one bit like them."

"I want to do more," she said, agony filling her eyes. "Moyra is captaining a ship in General Hackett's fleet. She needs a pilot."

Draif had to fight back his smile. He hated to lose her, but damn if he wasn't proud she wanted to be part of the fleet going to kill the Queen.

"Everyone thinks they're going on a diplomatic mission. They'll talk about you ditching your assigned ship to go on an easy assignment."

"Fuck them," she said, scowling. "I don't care what others think. I care about what I think is right. You're my captain, and I would never leave without your permission. That's why I'm here."

Draif pulled her into a hug. "You have my permission. I'm proud of you, Olla. Just let Moyra know she can't keep you."

She laughed against his shoulder. "Yes, sir."

They talked for a few minutes, then he walked her to the door. "I'll see you all off in the morning. Don't stop practicing your simulations. It will hopefully be a long, boring trip there, so take advantage of the time."

"I will," she said with a grin.

He shut the door behind her and sighed. Now he had to find a pilot to fill in until she returned. One that could keep their mouth shut.

"Fucking Ginger Telbea."

Wobble's head appeared through the open kitchen window, and he hummed a hello. A new scarf was wrapped around his neck, telling Draif Ava had been by to visit that morning.

"Hey, Wobble. Do you want some treats?"

Wobble clucked, almost sounding like he was agreeing.

Draif smiled and pulled some sliced apples out of the refrigerator. Wobble visited Sebastian and Draif daily to try to convince them Leti wasn't feeding him.

He fed the slices to Wobble, then washed his hands

before looking around the room. He found Marmalade sleeping in the kitchen window seat. He picked up the chubby cat and held her close. She blinked sleepily, then settled in, purring against his chest.

He slowly made his way to his office and made the call.

"Uh, hi, Captain Ando," Ginger said, looking a little afraid. "You know the other night wasn't a date, right? Lucas said he would make sure to tell you."

"I'm aware," he said, voice clipped. "You're between assignments now that you're back from Burnished Outpost, right?"

"Yeah. I'm on the waiting list to pilot for either the Blue or Yellow Fleet."

"Come to my house," Draif said, looking at the time, "about thirty minutes from now."

"It's next to General Hackett's house, right?" Her eyes looked like they were about to pop out of her face.

"Yeah."

"I'll be there. Uh, nice cat."

Draif ended the call and scowled as he checked his messages, petting Marmalade as she fell asleep in his lap.

One from Gus caught his attention, and his eyes widened. "Chad Ige. You really are surprising."

He sent a quick message, then went to his room to change his shirt. He wanted to look as professional as possible for his talk with Ginger.

He gently set Marmalade on the bed before pulling his shirt off. His reflection in the bedroom mirror caught his attention, and he studied himself. His hair really did look good. The gold beads made him look exotic.

He traced a hand over the dark rosettes that dotted his ribs and spread down his hips. A few, faint rosettes even lined the edges of his face. His Wello blood was much more prominent than Leti's, and he'd always been proud of his heritage.

His fingers trailed over his barely visible birthing line. "Marmalade, you'd like having kids around. Wouldn't you?"

He thought of a little girl or boy with Cardinal ears and a tail running around the house and playing with Leti's kids. They'd get into so much trouble together. Add in all the other neighborhood kids, and they'd probably destroy the station.

He had never given much thought to having kids of his own. He hadn't wanted them to be born into the mess that was Vextonar. Life was different now.

"Charybdis Station is a good place to raise kids," Draif said, looking over his shoulder at his sleeping cat. "You'd like to have a baby around, Marmalade."

His comm buzzed, and he saw that Ginger was walking up the path to his door.

He pulled his shirt on, then dropped a kiss to Marmalade's head before running down the stairs. Her knock came just as he reached the door.

Ginger looked a little baffled, standing on the doorstep. "This cat followed me up the walk."

Fluffle stared up at him, waiting for his permission to come inside.

He waved for both of them to enter. "Fluffle likes to visit Marmalade sometimes."

The fluffy calico went straight up the stairs, as if he knew where his friend was.

"Okay," Ginger said, stretching the word out.

He led her to the living room. "Sit. I have a proposition to make."

She snickered. "I don't think Lucas would like that."

Draif rolled his eyes. "Not that kind of proposition." He paced the floor in front of her. "I researched you, so I know you are an excellent pilot and loyal to the station. What I need to know is if you can keep your mouth shut about missions, meetings, and other business."

The amusement left her face. "Yes. I like my gossip, but I know when to stay quiet."

Draif sighed. "I need a pilot."

7

The next morning, Lucas patted Morgan's back as he hugged his friend. "I'll keep an eye on the girls. I know Wyatt's mom will take care of them, but Draif and I are right down the street too."

"Thanks." Morgan watched his adopted daughter Estella hug Wyatt. "It's hard to leave them, but I know this needs to be done. Don't let Estella run off and marry Mo while I'm gone. Also, Pela and Kiki are walking now, so make sure they don't run off to chew on strangers."

Lucas laughed. "Estella's just friends with Mo. She's not even a teenager yet. What the hell are you going to do when she *is* old enough to run off and get married?"

"Lock her in her room with Kiki and Pela. They'll guard her well."

Lucas felt odd staying behind while the others went away. He knew Draif had important things to do here, but it still felt wrong somehow.

Wyatt patted Morgan's back, then handed him Pela.

"Say goodbye before you scare Lucas away from having kids."

Lucas smiled, then hugged the young doctor. "Watch his back, Wyatt."

"I will."

Lucas let him go, then looked around for Draif.

His mate was standing with Hack and Leti's family as they watched Leti and Hack walk up the ramp to the Blue Solace. To most people, Draif would look calm and collected. Lucas knew him better than most. Draif was on the verge of a breakdown.

Lucas jogged over to stand beside him, nudging him with his shoulder. "They'll be back before we know it."

Draif swallowed and nodded. "Yeah."

Finn came to stand on Draif's other side. "Hack won't let anything happen to him, Draif. Leti is his heart and soul."

"He has Princess Buttercup too," Lucas added. "You know he will be anywhere Leti is."

"We've never been apart," Draif whispered. "From the day his dad brought me to him to right now. We've always been close to one another."

Finn wrapped an arm around Draif's shoulders. "I don't have any mushy words for you, but I know Leti will be back. You'll talk to him every day on the vidscreen. It's not the same, but it's something. They'll do their part, and we'll do ours."

Draif nodded. "We will."

Fasi and Renee came over. "Alright, kids. Let's get you all home. Moses is going to take you to the park after lunch."

Sami buried his face against Moses's shoulder. "Pax comes too, right?"

Moses stroked his head. "Yes. Your guardian is always welcome."

They started toward the tram, Fasi pushing the stroller with Pepper and Milo.

Alex, the eldest of Hack's younger siblings, stayed behind. "Draif, did Will get the chance to ask you?"

Draif smiled and nodded. "Yeah. Fasi is pushing the paperwork through now." He turned to Lucas. "Alex is going to be our newest soldier."

Lucas blinked. "You already finished basic training?"

Alex nodded. "We've been here for over a year."

"It doesn't seem like that long." Lucas shook his head. "We'll introduce you to the crew tomorrow morning and get you working with Ned and Crimson."

"Okay. I'll see you tomorrow." Alex rushed to catch up with the rest of his family.

Finn swallowed hard. "I promised Hack I'd keep Alex alive while he was gone."

Draif rubbed his eyes. "Me too."

Shae wandered over with Xu, Selene's son, and Nessa, Dannol's daughter. He carried Nettle and Lilah's daughter in his arms. He would be caring for all three while his sister and their friends were gone.

Shae looked around at them, then whistled loudly to get their attention. "Okay. We need to stay positive. Our families will be back soon enough. Follow me to Juniper's. I'm running the place while he's gone, and I want fried food, damn it."

"Uncle Shae, you aren't supposed to say bad words in public," Nessa said and took Shae's hand. "Come on. I'll tell you which words not to say."

Shae's brows rose. "You know them?"

"Yeah. Daddy and me practice cursing for when I grow up. He says it's important to get it right."

"Aww," Finn said, grinning. "Dannol is such a good dad."

Shae snickered. "Okay, Nessa. Teach me, wise one."

Lucas laughed. "Fried food and cursing lessons sound good. Come on."

Draif stayed close to his side as they walked to the tram, and Lucas had to fight himself to not put an arm around him.

"Have I told you your hair looks good?" Lucas said, hoping to distract Draif.

Draif rolled his eyes. "Only a thousand times. Leti made me promise to pick up some hair beads for Cas and Sami while we're on Derelict."

Lucas snorted. "That will make Cas happy. I guess we need to request another pilot. It will take some time, and we're scheduled for Derelict in two days. I'm not sure what to do."

Draif shrugged. "I could fly us if needed, but I got a pilot yesterday."

Lucas frowned. "You did? Why didn't you tell me?"

Draif made a face. "It's fucking Ginger Telbea."

"Seriously?" Lucas started laughing. "I bet that conversation was fun."

———

Later that night, Lucas struggled to fall asleep. He stared out the window at the darkened light of the station. The shields surrounding their mock planet shimmered with silver and gold lights. A few shuttles flew over the Blue Sector, their night lights glowing brightly as they zipped past.

The neighborhood was so empty, even though Ma and Pops were at Alois and Sebastian's house, Fasi and Renee stayed at Leti and Hack's place, and Shae had given up his apartment to move back into Selene's home while he watched over Xu, Sophie, and Nessa.

Most of the other houses were empty.

There was no Princess Buttercup marching down the walkway to Morgan and Wyatt's house. There was no Mustachio flying high above them, surveying the neighborhood and occasionally dipping down to terrorize them. Gravy and Periwinkle weren't in the long, open backyard, trying to make more puppies. Fluffle wasn't here to stop by and visit with Marmalade.

Hell, even Juniper's had lost some of its light. Miss Speckles wasn't sitting in her flower pot greeting the customers, and Porkchop wasn't ruling the backyard. Juniper wasn't there to greet them with a smile and a drink.

It was eerie and sad.

"Lucas?" Draif stood in the doorway, Marmalade in his arms. "Can I sleep with you tonight?"

Lucas patted the bed beside him, and Draif climbed in. They often fell asleep together, but this felt different.

Draif's eyes were vulnerable and sad.

"Leti isn't next door," Draif said softly. "It feels wrong."

Lucas leaned on his side and brushed Draif's hair back from his forehead. "You aren't alone. Leti isn't here, but I am."

Draif watched him, eyes dark with something Lucas didn't understand. "I've done something stupid, Lucas."

Lucas shook his head. "I can't believe that. You're too smart. I swear you dance around me, always a step ahead in everything."

Draif's laugh was wet and almost painful. "There are some things I'm not good at. When I was on Vextonar, the other slaves and servants called me cold and bitter. I didn't want to connect with anyone."

"After what Beldon Cortez did, I think that's understandable," Lucas said.

"I really did love him," Draif said quietly. "I try to tell myself that I didn't, but I did love the man I thought he was. As good as I am at reading people, when it comes to love, I'm oblivious."

Lucas's clawed fingers curled into the bed. He wanted to kill every last person who had ever hurt his mate. "You were only fifteen, and he was a manipulative bastard."

"Even when I met Leti, and I had as much freedom as he could give me, I wasn't like the others. I didn't usually care about men or women or sex. I didn't flirt or even notice most of the time when others were flirting with me. I knew sex. The training compound made sure of that. I didn't know love. Not outside of my love for Leti and his menagerie."

"There's nothing wrong with you," Lucas said. "Why do you think you've done something stupid? Did someone flirt with you and you didn't notice?"

That happened more often than Lucas cared to think about. If he could tattoo his name on Draif's forehead, he would do it in a heartbeat.

"No." Draif shook his head. "I fell in love."

Lucas's mouth was suddenly dry, and his heart might have stopped. "In love? With who?"

It better be me, he thought, claws tearing through the bedding.

"With my best friend."

Lucas sat up, snarling. "Leti? He belongs to Hack… No."

Draif rolled to his back and looked up at him, a small smile on his face. "No, idiot. Leti is my brother… *You're* my best friend."

Lucas opened his mouth, then shut it again. This was what he wanted. It was everything. Why couldn't he speak?

"I told you it was stupid," Draif said, burying his face against Marmalade's sleeping form. "I know you can have anyone you want. I won't make it weird, alright?"

Lucas lay back down and stroked Draif's beaded hair. "I've waited almost two years to hear you say you love me."

Draif looked up, tears in his eyes. "What?"

"I knew you were my mate the second we met,

Draif. Your scent is this crazy mix of sunshine and catnip. I knew you were mine."

Draif sat up, face angry. "Why the hell didn't you tell me?"

Lucas pushed himself up. "What would you have done?"

Draif shook his head. "I… Leti and Hack fell right in together. They fit perfectly."

"We did too," Lucas said, smiling. "As friends. I was afraid you would feel pressured to love me like that. I know you didn't see me that way, Draif."

Draif cried out, sounding like a wounded animal. "I would have tried to. I would have given you what you needed."

Lucas cupped his face. "You *have* given me exactly what I needed. You were my friend. You came to me when you needed to talk. You listened to me prattle on about everything. You helped me adjust to my new leg, arm, and eye. You let me move in and make your house our home. Hell, you watch my back while I have a monthly catnip day."

Draif snorted. "I love watching you and Finn on catnip. It's the funniest shit I've ever seen."

"Hey now, we have a lot of profound moments."

"You two talked for hours about how there are more nipples in the universe than people."

"Anyway," Lucas said, enjoying the sound of Draif's laughter. "What I'm trying to say is, you are exactly what I need. We aren't Leti and Hack, or any of the other couples in the neighborhood. We're you and me, and that right there is fucking perfect."

Draif reached up and rubbed one of Lucas's ears. "I didn't think of you sexually until a few months ago. Before that, you were just my Lucas. I knew I liked it when you touched me and slept beside me. I didn't like other people flirting with you, but I didn't think of you and me together like that. Then, one day the crew was sparring, and you looked at me like I was the most amazing thing you had ever seen. After that, you were sparring with Anders, and you took your shirt off. Your back was to me, and the muscles in your shoulders and ass were clenched as you blocked a kick. Suddenly, there was something else there. Something that took a fucking long time to build up."

Lucas grinned. "You like my ass?"

"I love your damn ass. It's yours, so it's the best ass in the galaxy."

Lucas laughed and pushed Draif back on the bed, letting his body settle on top of the smaller man's. "I love your ass too."

Draif stroked his cheek. "Good. Now kiss me."

Lucas pressed his lips to Draif's and let sensation take him away. Draif's taste was as good as his scent, and his tongue was warm and wet.

Lucas had sparred with Draif a thousand times. He'd hugged him and slept beside him. With their mouths pressed together like this, he had never felt so intimately close to his mate.

Lucas lifted his head and looked into Draif's dazed eyes. He wanted this man so much.

Draif shook his head and smiled shyly. "You'll hold me while we sleep?"

Lucas nodded and rolled to the side, Draif in his arms. "Yeah. Let's get some sleep. We'll talk more in the morning."

Marmalade curled up against his back, and Lucas was effectively wedged into place. His dick was hard as a rock, and he could feel Draif's erection against his stomach.

Draif smiled happily and closed his eyes, head on Lucas's shoulder and content to end the night with a kiss.

Lucas had never felt anything more perfect in his life.

———

THE NEXT MORNING, LUCAS WONDERED WHERE HIS perfect mate had gone.

Draif wore a forced smile and stood at the stove cooking breakfast, which he never did. "Good morning!"

"Okay." Lucas set Marmalade in the window seat. "What's happening here? You never cook breakfast. In fact, you're usually grumpy as hell in the morning and insist on having your coffee and some alone time with your tablet before you're able to act civilized."

Draif glared at him, cheeks flushed. "I can do better. I'll make breakfast in the mornings and get up earlier than you for my coffee."

Lucas gave him a baffled look. "Why?"

"Isn't that what you do when you're in a relationship? Think of the other person first?"

Lucas blinked. "Well, yes, but this seems weird. Hold on."

He grabbed his comm and called Morgan. His friend's face popped up on the screen.

"Wow, man. We aren't even out of the system yet," Morgan said, yawning. "What did Kiki do? She's our little troublemaker."

Lucas shook his head, then paused, thinking about it. "Well, I don't know. I haven't seen her this morning. She may have taken over the station by now. Who knows? We have a question for you."

"Okay." Morgan looked intrigued.

"When you're in a relationship, do you have to do things you wouldn't normally do just to make the other person happy?"

Morgan blinked. "Huh?"

Draif leaned over Lucas's shoulder. "Lucas and I are together now. Like *together* together. I think I should get up early and make him breakfast every morning."

Morgan blinked again.

"I don't think he should have to do that," Lucas said. "He isn't a morning person, and we have our normal routine. It's worked just fine so far."

Draif draped across his back and settled his chin on Lucas's shoulder. "So? What's the answer?"

"Uh," Morgan said. "Please hold while I transfer this call."

The screen went black.

"What just happened?" Lucas asked.

A second later, Hack's face popped up on the

screen. "Hey. Morgan said you have an important question? Are things alright at the station?"

Leti's face appeared over his shoulder. "What's wrong?"

"The station is fine," Draif said. "We have a relationship question. Should I cook breakfast for Lucas every morning and make an effort to not chew his head off when I wake up?"

"See, I think he's just fine the way he is," Lucas said, moving his head to kiss Draif's cheek.

Leti danced in the background, cheering and clapping, while Hack looked at them in confusion. "What the fuck?"

"Come on, Hack. You and Leti are the dream team," Draif said. "Give it to us straight."

Hack closed his eyes and swore under his breath.

The screen went blank again.

Draif curled his nose. "Is that asshole transferring us too?"

Nettle's confused face popped up next. "Hack said you two had a relationship question?"

Lucas sighed. "For the love of catnip. Should Draif have to change his normal routine just because he's in a relationship with me? A routine, I might add, that is just fine with me."

"Why are you asking me that? Aren't Ma and Pops two houses down from you both?"

"Nettle," Draif said. "Just answer the question."

Nettle's face disappeared, and Lilah's took its place. The Wello woman's expression was as solemn as usual.

"No. Draif should not force himself to become a

morning person unless he genuinely wants to. If your normal routine works for both of you, then there's no reason to change it up out of a sense of duty. You two work well together because you know one another so well and already consider how the other one feels. Just keep doing what you were doing before."

"Oh, thank the gods," Draif said. "I really don't like talking to anyone before the third cup of coffee."

"I really like getting breakfast ready," Lucas admitted. "I know it's just toast and fruit, but it's soothing."

Lilah shook her head. "You two are idiots."

The screen went blank, and Lucas shared a look with Draif. "We'll figure this out," he said. "We'll just take one day at a time."

8

THE BORAL SYSTEM, PLANET DERELICT

A few days later, Draif sat with Ginger and Brenna on the bridge of the Blue Raven. Lucas was with Crimson in the commons, and Anders was working with Ned and Alex. Tae was in his favorite spot of the ship – the engine room.

Draif stroked Marmalade's back. His cat was asleep in his lap, completely unconcerned with the galaxy. Draif liked knowing exactly where everyone was. He knew he was too controlling, but Hack told him he would loosen up once he'd been with his crew for a while.

This was their first extended mission together as a crew, and the three days they had spent together had gone a long way toward easing his mind. He knew he could trust these people. Even fucking Ginger Telbea.

The only downside was Lucas slept in his own quarters. Draif didn't know how to tell the crew he and Lucas were now a couple. At least, he thought they were a couple.

"Explain to me again why we're going to Derelict," Brenna said. The Siren sat in a padded chair next to him, ever-present tablet in her hands.

"This is supposed to be a simple errand for the Lord Admiral. You'll be buying things at the Trade Market."

Brenna rolled her eyes. "Yeah. I know what it's 'supposed to be,' though I don't know why *I* have to do the shopping."

He waved toward her. "You're fashionable and shit."

She gave him a flat look, and he squirmed in his seat.

She really is the stylish one on the crew, he thought. The Siren had dark purple skin and cropped light pink hair. She even had one of her horns pierced.

"Okay," she said, drawing the word out. "We traveled all the way from Charybdis Station so I can do some shopping. Oh, and I'm assigned to shopping duty because I'm beautiful and trendy."

"That's a very flimsy cover story," Ginger said. "Luckily, Derelict officials don't ask a lot of questions. They want our credits."

Brenna nodded. "True. So, what will you be doing while I'm shopping?"

"I'll meet with some contacts of mine to discuss strategy against HF."

She frowned. "That's what I don't get. Why not just have a chat on the vid-screen?"

Ginger winced, looking up from her control panel. "Some chats need to be in person."

Draif nodded in agreement. "I'm going to ask these

men to risk their lives to help us. It needs to be in person."

His comm chimed, and he answered it, handing Marmalade to Brenna and moving to the hallway for a little privacy.

"Hey Dottie." His friend looked tired. "What's wrong?"

"I have a favor to ask."

"Anything."

She smiled, eyes full of affection. "You're a good boy, Draif."

He flushed and cleared his throat. "What can I do for you?"

"I'm going to be sending a lot of folks to Charybdis Station."

Draif's eyes widened. "What happened?"

"There are rumors going around," she said, shaking her head. "The government isn't letting any civilian leave the planet, and word is, they're planning something big involving anyone not *pure* enough. Something terrible."

"You're smuggling people out?"

"Yeah." She sighed. "As soon as I can convince them, I'm sending my family too. My grandkids are hybrids, and my son and daughter are both just like me. We can't keep our mouths shut."

"You're afraid." Draif swallowed hard. "I didn't think you were afraid of anything."

"Vextonar has always been my home," she said. "My family has been here for generations. I love the damn polluted air and crowded walkways. It's not perfect.

Gods, it's as far from perfect as a planet can be, but I love it. I want it to be a better place."

"Your kids feel like that too. Don't they?"

She laughed, love filling her eyes. "Yeah. They're just like me."

"Then why send them away?"

"It's not safe here anymore."

"Send them to Charybdis Station, and I'll take care of them."

She smiled fondly. "Thank you, Draif."

"You'll come too. Right?"

She nodded. "When I've helped everyone I can."

Draif sighed in relief. "Good. I have a feeling HF will be working with Vextonar, and you don't want to get in their way."

"I need to get going," she said, then hesitated. "Draif. I'm sending some packages for you with my family. They're important. *All* of them."

He nodded. "Got it. I'll let the Lord Admiral know to expect arrivals."

He also needed to get moving to find the damn mole. Now more than ever, Charybdis Station needed to be a safe haven.

He went back to the bridge and watched through the viewport as they approached the small planet of Derelict.

Derelict was just as its name suggested. The planet was rocky, and the ground shifted constantly. Most man-made buildings didn't stay in place too long. The wealthier natives had compensated by using anti-gravitational tech for their more permanent buildings.

Homes and businesses tended to hover about a story above the ground. The less wealthy made do with dilapidated and crumbling buildings.

Draif linked his comm to the ship's communications. "Everyone report to the cargo bay once we've landed."

Ginger deftly maneuvered Draif's ship through the planet's atmosphere and docked on Derelict's largest hovering spaceport.

She frowned at the panels in front of her. "Captain, the spaceport official is asking our reason for being here."

"They didn't do that last time I was here."

"They've never done this," Ginger said. "I've docked here several times."

"Tell them we're visiting the Trade Market and refueling."

A moment later, she gave Draif a panicked look. "They want to know specifics."

Brenna gave him a sad look. "This is another effect of HF, isn't it? With so many planets devastated, even Derelict is being more selective of who they let on planet."

Draif closed his eyes. "I wasn't prepared for this. Hair beads? Leti wanted me to get them while we're here."

Ginger arched a brow. "They're not going to believe we came all this way for hair beads, and we don't need enough fuel to justify stopping just for that."

Draif made a face and thought for a minute. "Tell them we're searching for a Fire Veil Dragon. We aren't likely to find one here and that will give us reason to spend plenty of time on planet. Princess Buttercup is the most exotic thing I can think of."

"Got it," Ginger said, typing. She looked up and grinned. "We have permission to leave the spaceport."

Draif let go of the breath he was holding. "Good. Come on."

Once everyone was in the cargo bay, Draif gave his orders. Lucas wasn't going to like this.

"Tae, go ahead and refuel us while we're here. If we need any supplies, make it happen."

The sturdy hybrid nodded. "Got it, Captain."

"Ginger, as the pilot, you stay with the ship. Ned, you stay with her."

They both nodded, Ned looking disappointed.

"One of my contacts and his family are returning with us to Charybdis Station. His family will arrive while we're meeting. Ned, I need you to watch out for them. They've had a rough time and need a break."

Ned perked up. "Sure thing, Captain."

"Lucas, you and Alex will go with Brenna to the market. Our cover is that we're on a simple errand, but be sure to buy hair beads for Leti. Brenna knows what kind he requested."

Lucas narrowed his eyes. "I'm going with you."

"No," Draif said, meeting his mate's glare head on. "I need you ready to bring in backup if necessary. You and the rest of the crew are the only ones I fully trust on this planet."

Lucas gave him a pained look. "I love you, but right now, I wish you weren't so smart."

Draif hid his smile as the rest of the crew exchanged excited looks. He guessed he didn't need to think of a way to tell everyone.

"You finally made a move, Lieutenant?" Tae asked.

Draif sniffed. "Excuse me. *I* made a move. He would have waited an eternity."

Ginger snickered.

"Now, back on topic," Draif said. "Anders and Crimson will come with me. If things go south, contact Lucas immediately. I'm not expecting trouble, but Derelict's docking logs are public."

"Speaking of," Ginger said. "They asked for specifics when we landed. We told them we were looking for a Fire Veil Dragon. That's our story, so make it look good."

"They asked?" Lucas looked amazed.

"The officials here have good reason to be more cautious," Draif said. "All HF has to do is land a ship and the Queen can level the planet."

"Good point," Tae said, wincing.

"Let's go, people," Draif said, already wishing he was back home.

They split up as they reached the Trade Market, Draif exchanging a long look with Lucas. He knew Lucas was an excellent fighter and had a level head. He just needed to remind himself of that.

The market was full of visitors, just like the last time Draif was there. Now though, it was also full of armed enforcement officers. They watched the crowds closely, so Draif put a little swagger in his walk.

"Fuck, I could use a drink," he said.

Anders picked up quickly, and the blue Grell looked around. "There's this bar a couple streets over. It's called The Digger."

"They make a good drink," Crimson said, grinning.

They walked, didn't rush, and kept the conversation moving as they pushed through the crowds. Draif stopped by every table that sold pets and other animals, as if he were searching for a Fire Veil Dragon.

Eventually, they made it to the bar, and he led Anders and Crimson to the back corner.

"Crimson, stay here," Draif whispered. "If we aren't out in one hour, call Lucas. Anders, you're with me." He smiled coyly and grabbed Anders's hand. "Come on. I want to have a little fun."

Anders quickly covered his panicked look with a grin. "Sure thing, handsome."

Draif giggled and pulled Anders up the stairs, ignoring the knowing smirks the other patrons sent them. He pulled Anders down the hall, and they slipped into the last door on the right. The room was small, with a decent-sized bed in the middle and a table in the corner.

Gus was already there. The Dedril hybrid leaned back on the bed, his tablet in his hands. "Hey, the room is secure. We can talk freely."

Draif took the small black cube from his pocket and pushed a tiny button. It put off a very low frequency that should block anyone listening in. Just in case.

Gus nodded approvingly. "I like that model. Good choice."

Draif was glad the hacker understood his caution and didn't get defensive.

Chad Ige sat at the table with Zynzi Rainer, a Drellian shipping magnate. Since Ige was starting his own shipping company on Derelict, they would have plenty to talk about.

The last man in the room stood near the curtained window. Aiden Crow was one of Dottie's favorite contacts. He was a large, dark-skinned, mixed-species hybrid and a damn good smuggler. He also hated Humans First with a passion. Just like every other man in the room.

"You invited a human to this conversation," Crow said, nodding toward Ige.

Draif nodded. "Yes, I did." He looked around the room, noting the facial expressions and body language of each man. Crow was suspicious and looked about to cut and run. Ige was curious, but annoyed with Crow's behavior. Rainer and Gus both looked highly entertained by the whole thing.

Draif pulled his tablet out and pulled up a mobile scale of the known systems in the galaxy. He set it in the middle of the floor and stood. The systems spun in a slow circle, filling the center of the room.

"I have a proposition for you all. It concerns taking down Humans First and will require great risk on each of your parts. If you aren't interested, please leave now."

"How do you know we won't go right to HF and tell them Charybdis Station is planning something?" Ige asked.

Aiden snarled. "You're human. I still don't know why you're fucking here."

Draif cleared his throat. "Mr. Ige, if there is one thing I am completely certain of, it is that each of you hates Humans First with every bit of your being. Gus's family recently had to leave Rueal because the planet's government is becoming more sympathetic to Humans First every day. They're coming to Charybdis Station with me for a fresh start." Draif walked closer to the table. "Because of his shipping business in the Radiant System, Mr. Rainer and his company are directly in HF's path. They've already devastated two of the five worlds there. He is also on bad terms with Teresa Malone. To be blunt, the lives of both him and his family are at risk."

Rainer sat up in his chair, eyes narrowed. Draif knew the man had already received several death threats ordering him to close his companies.

Draif continued. "Crow's father was recently in the same situation as Rainer. He was the CEO of a small company on Rueal but was murdered so an HF sympathizer could take his place."

Crow gave him a hard look, then sank onto the end of the bed. From what Gus had dug up, Draif knew, despite their differences, Crow had been close to his father.

"What about him?" Crow asked, nodding to Ige.

"Mr. Ige is human and, to all appearances, on good terms with several members of HF."

Crow growled.

Draif settled his hand on Ige's shoulder and

squeezed. "However, two years ago, Mr. Ige was engaged to a Wello woman who was abducted, raped, and murdered by Harrison Goel and Sofus Hald on Vextonar."

Crow winced, but Ige remained stoic, eyes focused on Draif.

"I know each of you despise them and everything they stand for. What I don't know is how much each of you is willing to risk." Draif looked around the room. "What will it be?"

Gus winked, grin spreading across his face. "I'm in."

Crow nodded, eyes full of anger. "Me too."

Rainer smiled and saluted. "I want to see those bastards fall."

Ige leaned back in his chair. "Evelyn was my life mate. If there is any possible way to hurt them, I'm with you. What's your plan?"

9

Lucas walked beside Brenna, eyes scanning the crowds. Enforcement was keeping a close eye on everyone. His comm chimed, and Lucas read the message. Gus's family was aboard the ship.

One enforcer eyed them as he walked past.

"We have the beads," Brenna said, holding up a small bag for Lucas to see. "Now, to find us a Fire Veil Dragon."

The man nodded to them, then moved on to watch another group suspiciously.

A vendor started waving both his hands to get their attention. "Did you say a Fire Veil Dragon?"

Brenna hesitated and gave Lucas a questioning look, but the enforcement officer was back beside them.

"Yes, sir," Lucas said, smiling. "We're searching for a pet for my mate. He's convinced only a Fire Veil Dragon will do."

The vendor grinned. "You're in luck! Normally, you

won't see one of those off their home world, but a colleague of mine came across a hunter that sold him two babies. I couldn't believe it!"

The enforcement officer patted Lucas's back. "That is really good luck. I've never seen one in person, though I did watch a documentary on them once."

"She's two rows down," the vendor said, pointing behind him. "I'll let her know you're on your way."

"Do you mind if I tag along?" The enforcement officer gave him a hopeful look. "I want to see them."

Brenna laughed nervously. "Oh, surely you're too busy."

The man shrugged. "It's on my route. Come on, I'll show you."

"Thanks," Lucas said, smiling. Fuck him. He *did not* want two more Princess Buttercups.

When they reached the new vendor, the woman was practically vibrating with excitement. It looked like she was an exotic pet vendor, though there was the occasional dog and cat on display.

His eye caught on the three cages sitting side by side on the table in front of her space. Two of them held baby Fire Veil Dragons.

The first looked about the same size and age as Stardust. The filtered sunlight glinted off her dark-red scales. They varied from a rich garnet to a dark cherry red. Her big golden eyes watched Lucas, and she chirped a hello.

Curled around her was a large gray tomcat. The baby curved her head around to rest on the cat's back, eyes following Lucas's movements as he approached.

The second baby was older, not quite a juvenile. He barely fit in the cage. His scales were a mix of the darkest of reds, almost appearing black in places. His eyes were very similar to Princess Buttercup's – a bright yellow gold.

He hissed at Lucas. Yep. A lot like Princess. *Damn it.*

The third cage didn't hold a dragon. An odd purple, foxlike creature stared at him with shining blue eyes. His two tails whipped back and forth behind him.

Lucas smiled. He recognized the species from Beton. He was a Gelross.

He remembered something he had read in Captain Reed's dossier. "How much for all three?"

"The cat too," Alex said, pointing at the gray cat in the first dragon's cage.

―――――

LUCAS SHUFFLED HIS FEET AS DRAIF STARED AT THE cages in his bedroom on the ship. His tail swished in agitation. He didn't know if Draif was upset, happy, or gassy.

"I couldn't leave them there to be bought by some stranger," Lucas said. "They could have been hurt, abused, or even killed and mounted as trophies. The vendor said that was what happened to the dragons' mothers."

Draif pointed at the small stuffed toys Lucas had gotten for baby dragon one. They littered her cage. The baby's head rested on top of a stuffed orange cat that looked remarkably like Marmalade. Her gray tomcat sat behind her wearing a fancy jeweled collar.

"She looked lonely."

Draif arched a brow, then pointed at the jeweled collar.

"It's really stretchy," Lucas said hopefully. "He can wear it for a long time. Brenna picked it out. Just look at how it matches his fur. Don't worry. I got Marmalade one too."

Draif pointed at the second cage. The Gelross was curled up on a stack of soft pillows.

"Okay," Lucas said. "This one is a gift. Captain Reed's daughter loves animals as much as Leti does, and the Gelross are sweet companion pets."

Draif sighed.

"It's your fault for leaving his dossier where I could see it," Lucas said, scowling.

Draif came to stand next to the second baby dragon. He crossed his arms and eyed the young dragon that was *not* in a cage but, instead, was curled up on Draif's pillow.

Lucas held his hands up. "That cage was really small. I don't think this baby has learned to shift sizes yet. He's as big as a dog and doesn't need to be crammed into that tiny cage."

Draif sighed. "I love you."

"Really? You aren't mad?"

Draif moved and wrapped his arms around Lucas's neck, standing on his tiptoes. "How could I be? Now, get down here and kiss me."

Lucas growled and picked Draif up, bringing his

mouth to his. He let Draif lead the way, relishing his taste and the smaller man's hard body against his own.

Draif moved his hips against Lucas and pulled his mouth from his. "I want to touch you? Can I?"

Lucas swung him around and set him on the small table in one corner of the room. "Anything you want."

Draif smiled softly. "You. I just want you."

Lucas leaned forward and kissed Draif again. He felt Draif's hands drifting over his body, pulling his shirt off and unbuttoning his pants.

Lucas felt a twinge of self-consciousness when his robotic prosthesis was revealed. He had chosen not to hide it beneath reconstructed skin. Instead, it was solid black and chrome metal. He had nerves within it and could *feel* Draif's fingers run over the metal.

"Remember when you were first fitted with this?"

Lucas's laugh came out huskier than planned. "You made me walk around the house half-naked for months."

"You were so worried about how it looked." Draif ran his hands down Lucas's chest to the edge of his pants. "You wanted to be a badass and pretend like it didn't bother you, but I could tell it did."

"You don't mind it." Lucas knew Draif wasn't bothered one bit by his prosthesis.

"Nope. They're all just part of you. Hell, your eye is kind of handy to have."

Lucas laughed again. The doctors had fitted his eye with a scanner that he could activate if he ever needed to. Trust Draif to find it fascinating instead of weird.

Draif pulled him down for another kiss, this one

more heated. His hands ran over Lucas's shoulders, then back down his chest, before pushing his pants down his legs.

Lucas managed to toe off his boots and step out of his pants without falling over. "What are we doing, Draif?"

Draif tapped his chin, thinking. "First, you're going to fuck me. Then, you're going to go grab your shit and move into my quarters."

Lucas groaned and kissed him again. He had thought of this moment for a long time now. They would take it slow, and he'd get to taste every inch of Draif's body.

Draif bit Lucas's lip. "Now, Lucas. Fuck me now."

"Damn it."

Soon enough, Draif's pants were down his legs, and he was bent over the table with Lucas pushing into his ass.

Lucas pressed his cheek to Draif's, and they panted together as he pounded into his mate. He reached his hand around and took hold of Draif's dick, pumping it hard.

"Fuck," Draif gasped, shuddering when Lucas licked the side of his neck and bit down hard with his sharp teeth.

The taste of Draif's sweat and blood pushed Lucas over the edge, and he came with a long groan. He settled on top of Draif and continued pumping his mate's dick until he spilled all over Lucas's hand.

"You bit me," Draif said, wheezing. "Gods, that was good. It's never been like that before, Lucas."

Lucas started laughing, his body shaking against Draif's. "I had plans, you know. I was going to last hours. We were going to start off slow and kiss for a while. Then, I was going to suck your dick until you came down my throat. After that, I was going to taste every inch of you until you were ready to go again. At that point, I planned on slowly fucking you until you came again."

Draif pulled Lucas's arm under his head and relaxed into the table. He looked at his comm. "It's been ten minutes."

"Damn it!"

"We're a couple, right?" Draif's voice held a thread of uncertainty.

"Was I not clear? You're my mate, and I love you," Lucas said.

Draif kissed Lucas's wrist. "I remember what I felt the day we met. I knew you were important, that we would be friends. I didn't realize there would be a point when you were just as important as Leti. I don't want to lose you, and I know I'm not the easiest person to live with. I'm bossy and stubborn."

"You're driven to be the absolute best at everything," Lucas added, chuckling. "I don't just love you, Draif. I admire and respect you with every fiber of my being. Your fire is a beautiful thing, and I'm honored I get to stand at your side."

"What about sex? Sometimes I want it, sometimes I don't. As much as I love you, most of the time, I just want to kiss."

Lucas chuckled. "When you want to love on me, I'm

right here. When you don't feel like it, just let me hold you. You're it for me, Draif. Any bit of you I get is a treasure."

"That's the thing," Draif said. "I'll give you everything I have, but what if it isn't enough?"

Lucas kissed the back of his neck. "You are more than enough for me. Me and you? We're more than just fucking."

Draif was quiet for a minute. "Don't be mad. I swear I'm not trying to be confusing here, but how about you chase that dragon off my pillow and we give your plan a go? I'm definitely feeling the need for your dick inside me again. I want you to bite me again too."

Lucas laughed and stood straight. "My pleasure, Captain."

Draif stretched his back and eyed Lucas's naked body with a smile. "Good. Now, get to work."

10

ANCHORS REST SYSTEM, CHARYBDIS STATION

A week later, Draif sat in his office chair, Milo in his lap chewing his fist, while Sami sat in the window seat telling Pax a story.

Chad Ige's face was on one screen, and Aiden Crow's was on another.

"I'm in," Ige said. "The fuckers welcomed me with open arms. Apparently, they're preparing for something big and need as many ships as possible."

"Do Goel and Hald really not remember you?" Crow shook his head. "How can they murder a woman and forget about her fiancé?"

Ige's face turned dark. "All they knew was a non-human made a fool of them in public. Evelyn had a sharp tongue and didn't suffer fools. I suspect they didn't even know her name."

"Gus is working on hurting their pockets," Draif said. "I know that seems like poor revenge, but it's one step closer to defeating them."

Ige nodded. "One thing I noted already is that their

fleet is spread out. I've joined the largest one. It's gathered here at Rueal. A smaller force is somewhere in the Radiant System. I don't know where the third one is."

Draif nodded. "Thank you. I know this is risky for you."

Ige shrugged. "The captains in my fleet are all in. I would trust each one with my life, and they're a mix of species. They like the idea of taking HF down."

Crow's eyes widened. "HF doesn't mind having non-humans in their Fleet?"

"My ships aren't the only ones with a mix of species," Ige responded. "They pay well enough that the non-humans in their fleets set aside their morals."

Crow scowled. "Soon enough, the fuckers won't have the money to pay anyone."

"How's your rebellion going?" Draif asked.

"Plans are in place. I gathered who I can, but we could use more people," Crow said.

"I'll talk to the Lord Admiral," Draif said. "I'll see who we can send."

"Is Rainer having any success on his front?" Ige asked.

Draif laughed. "Yeah. He's working with Ava to smooth things over with the Drellian Chief."

A horrid smell started wafting up from Milo.

Draif's nose wrinkled. "I have to change this one's diaper. Keep me updated."

"Fuck," Sami said, waving in front of his face. "Milo made a big stinky."

Draif winced, and Crow and Ige laughed.

"You're such a good role model," Crow said, laughing as he ended the call.

Ige smiled at him. "I didn't know you had kids."

Draif shook his head furiously. "No, Lucas and I don't have any kids. These two cuties are my nephews. Their dad is on a mission."

Sami popped up beside him. "My daddies are making the galaxy safe for everyone. They'll be back soon."

"That's good to hear," Ige said, eyes soft. "Change that stinky diaper. I have one more bit of news."

Draif stood and quickly changed Milo's diaper. The little boy giggled as he played with his toes.

Draif sat back down. "What do you have?"

"Rumors," Ige said. "One of my captains was drinking with one of Cortez's men. He mentioned that Cortez and Malone both have the Equinox Assassins Guild on retainer. They're the ones that have been killing off the big four's competitors."

Draif pursed his lips. "That's not too surprising. They're the guild that tried to steal one of the Bracken."

"Here's the thing," Ige said. "This captain mentioned Cortez gave them a new job."

"Who? We can get this person some protection."

"Charybdis Station's Lord Admiral, Fasi Juren."

Draif's gut clenched. "I won't let them touch him."

"Good," Ige said. "Like I said, it was one conversation and a bunch of rumors, but I wanted you to be prepared."

When the screen went blank, Draif quickly called Finn and Bendix.

Finn smiled. "Hey, Draif."

Bendix smirked. "Uh oh. That's your serious face."

"I just got word the Equinox Guild is coming for Fasi," Draif said.

"I'll notify Renee," Finn said, smile gone. "We can increase security around his office and Leti and Hack's house."

"I'll notify his Half Moon guards," Bendix said. "He doesn't know they're there, but they follow his every move. Equinox isn't Half Moon, and they don't have our tech, but they're still competent assassins. You need to tell him."

"Thanks. I will," Draif said and ended the call. He rubbed his chest for a minute, trying to settle his worry.

"Are you sad, Uncle Draify?" Sami snuggled against his side. "Call Daddy."

"Good idea." Draif called his friend.

He wouldn't tell him about the threat to Fasi. There wasn't anything Leti or Hack could do, so there was no reason to worry them. Draif just needed to see Leti.

Leti's familiar face filled the screen, and Draif felt something settle in his chest.

"This is a pleasant surprise," Leti said.

"Daddy," Sami cried, hopping up and down. "Hi. Me and Milo are visiting Uncle Draify today."

Leti grinned. "Are you ready to start school tomorrow?"

"Yeah," Sami said, dancing in circles with Pax. "Grandpa Moses is gonna take me. He says Pax can't go."

"No pets allowed at school," Leti said, looking sad. "I always hated that part of school. You'll make lots of friends though, and Pax will be home when you get back."

Draif heard a squeak and looked toward the door. Honey, the youngest of the Fire Veil Dragons, carried a squeaky toy in her jaws. She watched him with bright golden eyes.

Lucas and Marmalade both loved her, and Draif had resigned himself to raising a dragon.

Chutney, the large gray tomcat, followed her into the room. At least they had his help with Honey.

"Hi Honey. Hi Chutney," Sami said and went to play with the baby dragon and her cat.

"Who're Honey and Chutney?"

Draif winced. "Two new pets. That's all."

Leti's eyes lit up. "You have more pets? It took forever for you to admit Marmalade was your cat."

"Chutney belongs to Honey, and I had to accept Honey. Lucas loves her."

Leti grinned. "And you love Lucas."

Draif grinned, knowing he looked like a lovesick idiot. "Yeah."

"You have no idea how happy that makes me, Draif," Leti said. "By the way, I liked your recent poem."

Draif had started to send Leti a poem about Lucas every time he received one from Leti about Hack. It was strangely therapeutic.

Leti rubbed his chin. "I never knew there were so many words that rhymed with loins."

Draif shrugged. "Writing poetry is a talent I never

knew I had. I liked your last one too. I never would have thought to rhyme tongue and well-hung."

———

LATER THAT AFTERNOON, FASI, RENEE, AND THE Council milled about Draif's living room, along with several other people. Draif was starting to realize his house really wasn't that big.

Lucas had a pouty Kiki strapped to his chest in a baby sling and worked with Draif to pass out drinks while they waited for the meeting to start. Draif had Pela strapped to him. It felt odd to have the warm weight of another person resting against his heart. It made his damn birthing line ache. He wondered if his and Lucas's baby would have his mate's dimple.

Draif cursed when the oldest baby dragon growled at Fasi when the Lord Admiral went to sit on Draif and Lucas's couch. He was a grumpy little snot.

"Good luck with him," Fasi said, eyeing the dragon.

"We're working on his people skills," Finn said. "He reminds me of a grumpy teenager."

"Honey is a sweet little girl," Lucas said, cooing at his dragon.

Honey curled up beside Marmalade and Chutney on a small pet bed near the window. Her favorite toys were scattered all over the living room floor.

"He isn't bad," Draif said, shrugging. "He's just grumpy. Kind of like Princess."

"Have you told Leti about them?" Pops grinned.

"You know he'll take both of them if you all didn't really want them."

Renee held her hand up. "No. Leti has too much to handle as is. I swear I don't know where he and Will find the energy to deal with Rizzie, Sami, Pepper, and Milo. Hell, Moses is always there, and Mo and Rose are the most helpful teenagers I know, but it's still exhausting."

Alex winced. "I can move back in if you need me to. I haven't really finished unpacking."

Renee leaned over to kiss his cheek. "No, sweetheart. You deserve the chance to spread your wings. I'm just complaining because I don't understand how Leti does it."

"Leti is used to taking care of a brood," Draif said. "He had plenty of practice with his menagerie on Vextonar."

"Speaking of the kids," Ma said from the window. "Here they come. They really shouldn't look that energetic."

Moses, Pris, and Ma's eldest daughter, Nala, had taken all the neighborhood kids to the park. Pela snuffled in her sleep, and her tiny fist clenched his shirt. Well, all the kids except Wyatt and Morgan's twins, Draif reminded himself, smiling gently.

Ma hadn't even finished speaking before Sami burst through the door, running straight to Draif. "Uncle Draify, I need hugs!"

Draif knelt and hugged him tightly, being careful of Pela. "Anytime, Sami boy."

"Can I visit with Honey, Uncle Lucas?"

Lucas nodded. "Just be gentle. She's napping with the cat nannies right now."

Sami let go of Draif and tiptoed to the sleeping cats and dragon. He slowly lowered to the floor and watched them.

Pax strolled in and went straight to Sami, settling in to watch Honey and Marmalade too.

Nala and Moses followed with all the other kids. *Damn there are a lot*, Draif thought.

"I'm just going to take these monsters to the backyard. I think the rest of your visitors are about to arrive," Nala said, shaking her head.

Pepper squealed, bouncing in her arms.

Nala set her down, and Pepper toddled straight to the older baby dragon and did her best to hug him. The dragon looked puzzled but let the little girl pet him.

"Mine." Pepper grinned, looking around the room. "Aagy mine!"

Renee groaned. "Why, Lucas? Why did you do this to us?"

Draif knelt beside Pepper and the dragon. "His name is Aagy?"

"Aagy." Pepper hugged the dragon again. "Come play!"

Nala laughed as she herded the children toward the kitchen. "Pepper is just like Leti. I almost feel sorry for Hack."

Aagy walked beside Pepper, letting the little girl balance herself on his side as she followed the others into the kitchen.

Draif heard a crash and giggling. "Why are we doing this at my house?"

Fasi snorted. "I don't have the energy to clean up after any more people. Renee is right. Leti and Will make it look so easy."

Pris came in, her son Darya on her hip. Her Fyrling, Siri, perched on her shoulder. "Your guests look a little nervous out there."

Draif shrugged, unconcerned.

"Bendix is on his way," Pris said. "He's bringing the, uh, item you requested."

Lucas tilted his head, curious. "Someone's head?"

She snorted. "You wish. Bendix has been trying to find one of Beck's Fyrlings a home ever since Beck and the Guild Master left."

Draif smiled smugly. "I have the perfect person in mind."

Ma shook her head, still staring out the window. "Those poor folks are all discombobulated. I'm going to get them."

Fasi gave Draif a look. "You sure about this?"

He nodded. "They can be trusted. Plus, I have animals to distribute."

11

Ma led Yeardley, Wyther, and Reed into the house. They looked disconcerted to find the Council and Lord Admiral sprawled about the room.

The three captains' families trailed behind them.

Yeardley's wife smiled sweetly and waved. Their Dedril daughter looked familiar.

"Draif?" The little girl darted over. "Remember me?"

Draif smiled softly. She was one of the original children he had helped rescue from the Concords. He had boarded the enemy ship to save Lucas but had found several prisoners.

He let her hug him. "I do remember. How are you, Coni?"

The little Dedril hugged him tightly. "Really good! Mama and Mommy are the best. I have classes with Nessa, and she said Wobble lives in the backyard."

"He does," Draif said. "I'm sure he'd like to see you

again. Ma could bring you to him. Nessa is in the backyard too."

Ma grinned. "If you kids want to come with me, I'll introduce you to the others."

Wyther's two sons went right with her, along with Yeardley and Wyther's wives.

Reed's daughter stood frozen in place, eyes wide and focused on the Gelross sitting alone at the bottom of the stairs.

"Daddy, look," the little girl said.

"Go on to the back with the others, Herma," Reed said, eyeing the Gelross.

Herma ignored him and ran to the pet, throwing her arms around him. "Hi, baby. I'm Herma, and I'll be your friend."

The Gelross stood perfectly still, eyes going to Lucas. Draif swore the animal looked panicked.

Lucas grinned and nodded at the Gelross, and the animal's eyes closed. He sank into the little girl until his head rested on her shoulder. A rumbling purr filled the air.

"He doesn't have a name yet," Draif said, ignoring Reed's headshakes. "He needs a good home. Someone to love him and raise him."

Reed's face went slack. "No!"

Herma squealed. "You can come home with me, baby. Do you like tea parties? Mine and Daddy's house has a big yard, and we can play chase. I'm a fast Grell, but I'll go slow if you can't keep up. I have a puppy and a kitty too. You'll like them. They can be your brother and sister. Daddy won't let me have a brother or sister 'cause he says he's never getting married again."

Reed's shoulders slumped. "Herma, you really don't want another pet."

She turned her little purple face to him, eyes big and sweet. "I love him, Daddy, and you said true love lasts a lifetime."

Reed glared at Draif. "Do you know what you've done?"

Draif grinned. "Found an orphaned baby a good home with a sweet friend and an honorable new dad?"

Pris struggled to hide her laughter. "Come on, Herma. Let's bring your new pet out back and show him off to the other kids."

"Okay. Come on, baby." Herma skipped toward the door, the Gelross following her with a tiny yip.

"Damn it," Reed said, glaring. "Why didn't you give it to Yeardley's daughter? Coni doesn't have any pets."

Yeardley snickered.

The door opened, and Bendix slipped in, something bulky in his arms. His Fyrling followed behind him. Murphy looked like a metal hippogriff, an Old-Earth mythical creature.

Draif cleared his throat. "I have other plans for Yeardley. Did you bring him, Bendix?"

"Sure thing, Draify," Bendix said and handed Draif a large metal toad. "Here you go." Bendix sat beside Renee, arm going behind her on the couch. He wiggled his eyebrows. "Hey lovely."

Murphy flew to the back of the couch, prancing around and shaking his head.

Fasi growled and stood, moving across the room to push Bendix over and sit next to his wife. "Watch it, assassin. I can still hold my own in a fight."

Draif admired the toad. It was the last of Beck's current Fyrlings. The creature was about the size of Draif's head and a mix of gold and emerald metals. Two thin and delicate looking metal wings lay flat against its back.

Black eyes watched him curiously, but the Fyrling must not have been impressed. It hopped out of his arms, flying straight to Yeardley.

She yelped but caught the creature, eyes wide.

Bendix looked at Draif. "She's the one you were talking about, right? Beck will kill me if I send one of his Fyrlings home with a shitty person."

Draif snorted. "She's good."

Bendix grinned at Yeardley. "Treasure him always, or the Half Moon Guild will make you wish you were dead."

Yeardley's eyes softened. "He's so pretty. I'll take good care of him. I promise."

"At least it's not a dragon," Draif said, shrugging.

Lucas stood and pulled him into his arms. "Sorry, love. Marmalade, Chutney, and I will raise Honey. I know you didn't plan on her staying with us."

Draif leaned up and kissed Lucas's chin. "I never said I wouldn't help with her. She's part of our family now."

Almost every person in the room stared at them in shock.

"When did this happen?" Fasi looked angry.

Draif blinked. "Honey? You know she came back with us from Derelict."

Fasi growled. "No, when did you two become a couple?"

"Right before we went to Derelict," Lucas answered, puzzled. "Are you angry?"

"Yes," Fasi said. "We've had a bet running for almost two years now. I had money on you two taking another three months."

Reed's mouth dropped open. "You bet on their love life?"

Wyther looked curious. "Who won?"

Councilwoman Rundel grinned. "That would be me, youngsters. I noticed the way Draif here started staring at Lucas's ass every chance he got."

Pops clapped. "Ma and I lost out, but we'll be throwing you a mating party. Just you wait!"

Draif's face flushed hot. "Okay. Let's get this meeting started."

Trixie chose that moment to walk out of the kitchen and up the stairs.

"Was that a goat?" Yeardley asked, eyes dancing with laughter. She held her Fyrling close to her chest, stroking its back.

Draif sighed. "Someone left the back door open. Okay, so ignore the goat." He moved to the front of the room. "First, thank you for meeting here. I know a conference room would be less chaotic, but until we catch the mole, this is the best place."

"Mole?" Reed's eyebrows rose.

Fasi nodded, unhappy. "Someone in my office is

feeding information to HF. That's why we're meeting here instead."

"It's also why we asked you to bring your family with you," Renee said. "We want this to look like a friendly get-together."

Councilman Mitchell grinned. "Our families are already back there too. My wife is liking the subterfuge a little too much."

"I have an idea on how to catch the mole, but I think we should let it go a little longer," Draif said.

"If there's a mole, why do you want to wait to find him?" Wyther said. "I would think you'd want that taken care of quickly."

Councilman Delino looked confused. "Very good question. Draif?"

"I want to feed the rat poison to take back to his nest," Draif said, voice hard. "I want HF to think we are as weak and helpless as possible. That means keeping them in place a little longer."

Fasi nodded. "Permission granted. Do you know who it is?"

"Not yet, but I'm hoping Reed here can help me figure it out," Draif said.

"How?" Reed looked confused, but willing.

"It's no secret you three don't approve of me," Draif said.

"What? Why not?" Fasi frowned at the three captains.

Draif waved away his questions. "It doesn't matter, Lord Admiral. I've played along with it for a while in case we got an opportunity like this."

"So, it's known Reed doesn't trust you," Finn said. "How does that help?"

Draif smiled. "He'll leave here upset with me and have a conversation with my three most likely suspects, letting them know he is privy to the Lord Admiral's plans."

"Well, you did give my daughter another pet, so I *am* upset with you," Reed said. "It shouldn't be too hard to be convincing."

Draif smiled sweetly. "Not sorry. Your daughter reminds me of Leti, and he's a good pet parent." He turned back to the others. "We'll figure out for sure who the mole is, then drop some information to them when we need to."

Fasi leaned back, impressed. "I like it."

Draif nodded. "Also, I've placed *my own* mole into the upper ranks of HF's coalition. I've already received updates on their movements and plans."

Fasi nodded, face troubled. "Bendix told me about my new guards. Are you sure it's necessary?"

"We knew they'd turn their eyes to us sooner or later," Renee said, settling her head on Fasi's shoulder. "It makes sense they'd try to take you out first."

"What?" Reed's face turned dark. "HF is targeting our Lord Admiral?"

Draif nodded. "The Equinox Assassins Guild will try to kill him. We won't let them succeed."

"Damn right we won't," Bendix said, bristling.

Draif rubbed his face. "Now, Ava and I have some updates for you."

Ava stood and smiled. "It's been confirmed that

Rueal has fully allied with Humans First. It's not official, but it's a done deal. HF is using the planet as a gathering place for its fleets and a central hub for command."

"I have no doubt Vextonar will join them soon," Draif said. "We have refugees arriving within the week. Dottie has been smuggling folks out as quickly and quietly as she can."

"What can we do?" Councilman Warren said. The Havonite looked tired.

Ava grinned. "We attack them where it hurts – their pockets."

"I've been working with a hacker," Draif said, bumping Ava's shoulder with his. "We're steadily draining their accounts and transferring credits into one large, hopefully untraceable, account."

Gus was really good at covering his tracks, but Draif knew no one was infallible.

"How much have you taken?" Councilman Delino leaned forward, ears twitching atop his head.

"In the past week, we've reduced their cumulative accounts by twenty percent. My contact says by the end of next week, they'll be down by fifty."

"They don't know where it's going?" Renee looked shocked.

Draif shook his head. "Not at this point. We're hoping to get more before we have to switch up tactics."

Yeardley, Wyther, and Reed stared at him in shock.

"This is what you've been working on?" Reed asked.

"All those times we've been bothering you about training, you've been doing this?"

Draif nodded. "Granted, it's not like I'm the one doing the hard work."

Reed just looked at him.

Ava patted Draif's back. "The Lord Admiral and I will meet with the Queen of Siren's Lament, the Dedril King of Aruta, and the High Chief of Drell. I'll need Cas to be there too."

Councilman Mitchell's eyes widened. "We haven't been on good terms with the Drellian Chief for a while."

Ava shrugged, eyes hard. "It's time to change that. They're a large presence in the Radiant System, and we need that." She linked her arm with Draif's. "Tell them what else you're working on, darling."

Draif smiled at his friend. "I'm also working with a group of rebels to sabotage HF's production factories. We want them as weak as possible when they come. Lord Admiral, I've provided you the details. Would you consent to send a couple of our crews their way? They could use more people."

Fasi nodded.

Yeardley arched a brow. "Let me guess, there's a reason you invited me and Wyther today too?"

Draif shrugged. "I don't know each and every captain on the station, but I know enough of you three to be certain you are loyal and trustworthy, as well as competent. I'm basically handing you the lives of the rebels I'm working with. If they're discovered, they'll be killed."

Fasi gave them a curious look. "How about it, captains?"

Yeardley nodded. "I'm in."

"Me too," Wyther added. "We won't let you down."

"It will involve a lot of traveling and probably take a few months," Draif said. "Of course, it'll also be extremely dangerous. You'll be traveling in enemy territory."

"We're glad to help," Yeardley said. "HF needs to go, and destroying their physical resources will hurt them."

Draif nodded. "It'll take a little time to get everyone in place, but we want to have multiple, simultaneous attacks. Once one factory goes, security will get a lot harder to bypass. Our hope is, with one swoop, we can cripple them. Hald and Cortez are the industry lords, but Goel and Malone rely heavily on them. If our plan works, all of Hald's and a good third of Cortez's factories will be out of commission."

"What's the timeline on this?" Fasi asked.

"My contact says it will take about a month to finish setting up. That will give Yeardley and Wyther time to get to their separate locations and provide manpower," Draif said.

Councilman Delino rubbed his chin. "What if we sent more than Yeardley and Wyther's crews?"

Draif did his best not to bounce in place. "The plan is to attack all at once, then get the hell out of there. The more people we send, the more factories we can hit."

Fasi smiled slowly. "Audre, my dear. Would part of

your fleet be up to helping a few rebels blow things up?"

Draif bit his lip. "They need to be completely trustworthy, Audre. Like I said, if the rebels are discovered, they're dead."

The Yellow General nodded, then smirked. "I can already think of a good dozen captains that will want in on this. They're all men and women I would trust with my life."

Cas pouted. "What about my fleet? Why can't we help blow things up?"

Ava gave him a sympathetic look. "Oh, don't you worry, sugarplum. Your fleet will be plenty busy. So will Sheiria's."

Finn opened his mouth, and Draif shook his head. "The Blue Fleet has a job too, so no, you can't go blow shit up."

Finn's ears flattened. "Rude."

Draif noticed Sami still sitting next to the cat bed. The little boy watched him with big eyes. He reached down and picked him up, hugging him tightly, Pela sandwiched between them. They had to get this right.

Councilman Mitchell shook his head. "This is really happening, isn't it? Those bastards are finally going to pay."

wo weeks later, Lucas sat on the floor of the living room with Rizzie playing tug-a-war with Honey. A tiny puff of smoke came from her nose as the little dragon bit down hard on one end of the rope.

Rizzie smiled, but her eyes were sad.

"You missing your dads?" Lucas asked.

She nodded. "I know they'll be back, but I miss them a lot. I even miss Daddy Leti's cooking."

"You talk to them every night, right?"

She nodded again. "It's not the same."

"Knock, knock," Pops called out from the front door. "Can we come in?"

"Sure, Pops. We're in the living room."

The large Grell carried a load of piping and rolled a Druffle hutch behind him. "We have a present for my Draify loo."

Mo followed him in, arms full of piping and a large tool pack strapped to his back.

Lucas fought a grin. "Let me guess. Some of Leti's Druffle?"

"Yep. They're outgrowing their hutches, and we need to spread them around some. Draif spends so much time in his office, so I'm gonna put some Druffle there. They'll keep him company, so he won't get lonely."

"I'm sure he'll appreciate it." Lucas *was not* sure Draif would appreciate a wall full of Druffle tunnels, but there was no way anyone could say no to Pops. His cute green face would get all sad.

"I'll get started then." Somehow, the Grell managed to carry the tubing and hutch up the stairs.

Rizzie started giggling. "Uncle Draif can't even get mad. He loves Grandpops too much."

Lucas laughed with her. "You're not wrong, ladybug."

Draif came in, Sami on his back. "Gus just called. HF finally managed to kick him out of their accounts."

"How much did he get?"

"All together, about sixty percent of their combined assets," Draif said with a grin. He ran around the room, Pax at his heels while Sami giggled from his back.

"Stage two?"

"The big four's names are being plastered on every news site across the galaxy as we speak," Draif said.

His second plan of attack was to release every shred of evidence Gus had gathered to the public. Lucas had watched him send the files that morning.

"How's the public taking it?"

Draif sighed. "They're shocked. I don't get it. HF claimed ownership of the destruction of Union Station. They publicly applauded each and every one of Air's victims. Yet, somehow, people are still shocked to find out that HF has been behind every single attack."

"People don't want to believe," Lucas said. "If they acknowledge it's happening, then they have to do something about it."

Draif spun Sami around and set him down on the couch. Pax hopped up to circle the boy.

"Shae's bringing his bunch over for dinner tonight," Draif said.

"I'll cook," Lucas said, letting the tugging rope go. Honey fell on her butt and rolled over. She looked at him and huffed out a little spiral of fire.

Draif laughed until he snorted. "Fuck, she's so cute."

"Uncle Draif," Rizzie said, gasping. "You shouldn't say bad words. Daddy Leti will get mad at you and take away your toys."

"If you say fuck at school," Sami said, laying his head on Pax's side. "They call Grandpa and tell him you're being bad."

Draif looked at Lucas, eyes full of laughter. "Remind me to clean up my language before we decide to have kids."

"Hmm," Lucas said, hiding a grin. "How *is* school going, Sami?"

Sami pulled Pax's tail around and started chewing on it, careful not to bite too hard. "It's okay. They makes you sit a lot, but then we get to play."

"Tell them about Almond," Rizzie said, grinning.

"Almond? Like the nut?" Draif asked, brow furrowed.

"He's not a nut. He's my friend," Sami said. "He's smaller than me, so I watch out for him. Then, when it's time for numbers, he helps me."

Rizzie giggled. "They call him Almond because he loves them. He carries them around and eats them all the time."

"It's 'cause he's small and needs to eat lots," Sami said. "There's nothing wrong with him."

"I know," Rizzie said, rolling her eyes.

"Hey," Shae called out from the door. The slender Siren had Sophie balanced on his hip. Xu and Nessa followed.

"Xu," Rizzie said, jumping up.

The kids settled down on the floor to play with Honey while Lucas led Shae and Draif to the kitchen.

"How's Fasi?" Shae said. "I hate that he has to stay at his office all the time."

"Just until the assassins are caught," Draif said. "Renee is working with Enforcement to catch them at the spaceport, and Reed and I have figured out who the mole is. I think they'll ask his help to get the assassins into the station."

"Then we get the mole?" Lucas pulled out some vegetables and started chopping.

"No, then we use the mole to send false information to HF," Draif said. "Enough with that business. Shae, why haven't I seen Liam with you the last few times you've visited?"

Liam Doney was an excellent pilot for the Blue Fleet, and he had been dating Shae for a while now. The man wasn't around all the time, but he'd come to several get-togethers with Shae in the past.

Shae's cheeks flushed with anger. "Liam didn't agree with my choice to watch over Xu, Nessa, and Sophie while their parents are on a mission. He said I shouldn't put my life on hold."

Draif scowled. "How is watching the kids putting your life on hold?"

"It's not. I run a daycare," Shae said, rolling his eyes. "Hell, taking care of Juniper's diner is a bigger shift in my life than the kids."

"What's his problem then?" Lucas asked.

"He finally admitted he doesn't like kids," Shae said. "The problem is that *I do* like kids. Eventually, I want a family of my own, and Liam doesn't. Watching Xu, Nessa, and Sophie just brought the issue up."

"Maybe he'll change his mind," Draif said, giving Shae a strained smile.

Shae snorted and set Sophie down so she could toddle around. "He's already dating someone else."

Lucas's ears flattened. "I think I need to have a talk with the fucker."

"Fucker," Sophie said, little face wrinkled up in a glare.

Shae gave him a horrified look. "What is wrong with you?"

Draif laughed. "It's probably a good thing Lucas and I don't have kids."

Lucas went back to cooking dinner.

"Speaking of kids, where are the rest of Leti's?" Shae asked, yawning as he sat at the table.

"We split them up for the night to give Grandpa Moses and Renee a break," Draif said. "Milo and Pepper are with Ma and Pops, and Rose went to stay the night with Sebastian's sisters. Mo should be here soon. He's going to bring his rabbit and stay the night with us. He wanted to meet Chutney and Marmalade."

"Leti being gone feels so strange, doesn't it? I keep expecting to see him walking through the neighborhood with everyone in tow. Everything is so quiet," Shae said.

"It is," Lucas agreed. "Soon enough, everyone will be back, and the neighborhood will be loud and obnoxious again."

Pops and Mo came into the kitchen. "Everything is set up. I'll bring the Druffle by in the morning?"

Draif blinked. "Huh?"

Pops hugged Lucas's mate, lifting the small man off the ground. "You're getting some of Leti's Druffle. That office of yours is too quiet. They're good little critters and can keep you company."

"Thanks, Pops," Draif said.

"Anything for you, Draify loo." Pops set him on his feet, then went out the back door with Mo.

Draif glared at Lucas.

Lucas shrugged. "It wasn't my idea, love."

Draif's communicator buzzed. "I'll be right back."

Shae watched him go, then turned back to Lucas. "Okay, so you two are life mates and officially a couple now. When is the wedding?"

Lucas gave him a flat look before getting out the chicken. "I'm not pushing him, so don't you go teasing us.

Shae bit his lip. "It's what I do though. I can't promise anything."

Draif came back in, face pale and eyes dull and lifeless.

Lucas dropped the knife and ran to his mate. "What's wrong?"

"Gus sent me this. The woman is President Wineon of Vextonar." He held up his comm and a video played.

"Thank you for joining us today. I will attempt to keep this brief. Vextonar is one of the best, if not the best, planet in the galaxy. We pride ourselves on our purity, intelligence, and wealth. As the President of Vextonar, I have worked with our Congress of Prime to bring our planet to the next stage of greatness. Today, Vextonar is pleased to announce we are joining the renowned coalition, Humans First."

The woman held her hands up again.

"Please, no questions. The Prime of Vextonar recognize greatness can only be achieved when we 'cut the fat away.' Last night, all citizens that were not at least eighty percent human were arrested. We don't want our planet to be the home to lesser species.

"Our dear friends in Humans First suggested we rid the galaxy of these mutts, but we've chosen to show mercy. We have sold these lesser species and hybrids, so they can serve a greater purpose. If you wish to purchase one, please contact the Vextonian embassy on your planet."

Shae covered his mouth. "Oh gods."

"During the gathering last night, we made some horrible

discoveries. Some humans, pure humans, were committing treasonous acts against our species by aiding the filth that has plagued our planet."

Behind her, seven people were led out of the building. They each had their hands tied behind their backs.

"Isn't that…" Lucas met Draif's eyes.

"It's Dottie," Draif said, voice empty of emotion.

"For their crimes, they will be publicly executed. We will not stand for treason against our great planet."

Dottie pushed forward, shouting. *"This isn't about Vextonar. It's not about humans. It's about greed and cruelty. You've sold over sixty percent of your population into slavery. That's treason, you stupid bitch. If you think all of humanity will let you get away with this, you underestimate us."*

The woman nodded to the guards. *"Kill them."*

Each guard pulled a phaser and shot a prisoner in the back of the head. Dottie's body crumpled to the ground.

Shae shook his head, tears streaming. "Her daughter just got here two days ago. I met her at the spaceport. Dottie's son is arriving tomorrow. They expected their mother to follow them."

Draif walked into Lucas's arms and pressed his face into Lucas's shoulder. "I need to let Lacey know Dottie is dead."

Lucas wrapped him in his arms. Draif's body shook, but he didn't cry. Lucas's stubborn mate refused to cry.

"I'll finish dinner and watch the kids," Shae said. "You two go to her family."

———

D OTTIE'S DAUGHTER, LACEY, CRIED AGAINST HER husband's shoulder. Dottie's son hadn't reached the station yet. Abe had sent his family with his sister and was escorting several more people to Charybdis.

They would reach the station tomorrow.

"I'm so sorry, Lacey," Draif said, voice harsh. "I should have seen this coming. I should have checked up with her again and pushed her to get out of there."

Lacey started laughing even as she cried, on the edge of hysteria. "Abe and I knew this would happen. My gut told me she'd stay behind, even if she said she'd follow after us. There is nothing you could have done to convince that stubborn woman to leave her planet."

Draif closed his eyes, face worn and strained. "I'll make Humans First pay."

Lacey wiped her eyes and leaned against her mate, a young Dedril. "I have every certainty you will. Mom adored you, Draif. She was so proud of everything you accomplished while you were on Vextonar." She started crying again. "Do you know how often Mom would use you to motivate Abe and me? She would say, '*Draif just finished training in land-battle strategy, and you got suspended for making out with a boy in the school restroom.*'"

Draif blinked. "That can't be right. We only saw each other a few times a month after I was sold to Leti."

Lacey reached out and took his hand. "She loved you, Draif. She tried to buy you so many times when you were a kid. Then, when you went to Leti, she checked in as often as she could. I feel like I know you and Leti with how much she talked about you."

Draif shook his head. "That can't be right."

Lucas wanted to cry. His mate had to know that woman loved him. Lucas had heard several of their conversations, and he could see it himself.

Lacey wiped her eyes again. "I know you and this station will do everything you can to defeat HF."

"We will," Lucas promised.

Lacey's eyes grew hard. "I want to be right there when you do, Draif. Do you understand me? I want to see you crush them."

Draif nodded. "If that's what you want."

She swallowed and nodded. "Abe will too. Damn it. I need to call him."

Lucas stood with Draif. "If you need anything, please let us know."

She smiled and patted his arm. "Mom knew about you, Lucas. She would have been so happy Draif and you finally figured things out."

Lucas swallowed hard. "I think so too."

They left the temporary house Dottie's family was living in, and Draif sank into his side. "Dottie is dead, Lucas. She's gone. Vextonar doesn't have a guardian anymore."

Lucas didn't like the hollowness in his voice. "I know she meant a lot to you."

Draif shook his head. "I was just a slave. I couldn't love her. I couldn't have her."

"Draif," Lucas said, tilting his head up. His mate's eyes were glassy.

"She wasn't mine. She couldn't be. Dottie was a… a burning warmth, Lucas. She held that place together and offered safety to everyone, not just the Prime caste. The bastards just shot her, like she was nothing. Like me. They took that light away."

Lucas held him tightly.

"Dottie was like Leti," Draif said quietly, face buried against Lucas's shoulder. "She was fucking brilliant and full of love. She would pull people to her and make them family."

Lucas couldn't stand this. He had never seen Draif so shaken up. After a few minutes, Draif pushed back, out of his arms, and his hollow eyes sent a shiver down Lucas's back.

"Come on," Lucas said and tugged Draif behind him.

"What? Where are we going?" Draif asked.

Lucas ignored him and sent a quick message to Bendix and Finn.

When they reached the tram, Lucas pulled his mate into his arms and pressed Draif's head against his chest. "I can deal with mad, Draif. I *can't* deal with you feeling like you're nothing."

"I am nothing. I just sit in my office and scheme," Draif said. "It didn't save Dottie or Vextonar and Rueal."

"Draif, there is only so much one person can do. It's okay to grieve her. It's okay to be angry."

"Sometimes I feel so much inside," Draif said, voice empty, "but it's like it gets stuck. There's no reason for it, so there's no way for it to come out."

Bendix and Finn met them at the shuttle tram in Half Moon's neighborhood.

"What are we doing here?" Draif asked, voice sullen.

"Bendix here has ten Half Moon assassins that can't wait to kick your ass," Finn said. "I called in your crew and a few other folks to stand with you."

Draif shook his head. "What are you saying?"

Bendix's Fyrling flew to Draif's shoulder and nuzzled him.

"It's time to get mad, Draif," Bendix said. "Humans First killed a person you loved."

Draif shook his head. "No."

Lucas pulled him toward Half Moon's training compound.

Fasi, Renee, and Draif's crew waited with Bendix's people. They all wore their training clothes.

"This isn't necessary," Draif said.

Fasi pulled him into a big hug. "Oh, my sweet boy. This is very necessary."

Renee hugged him from behind. "A good sparring match is just what you need. It'll settle that buzzing head of yours and give you something to focus on."

Ginger bounced in place, fists raised. "Come on, Captain. Now's the time to kick my ass like I know you want to."

Bendix waved to his group. "Don't hold back, Half Moon. Draif's a biter."

———

Several hours later, Lucas collapsed onto the couch. Every bone in his body hurt, and he was exhausted.

Marmalade and Chutney gave him sympathetic looks from the windowsill. Honey chirped at him and crawled up his leg to settle on his chest. She tilted her dark red face and studied him.

Draif leaned over him from behind the couch. "Are you alright? Otto has a mean right hook."

Lucas smiled. "I got him back. I don't think he knew my arm was robotic."

"Ginger was a surprise. I didn't know she could move that fast," Draif said.

"I can't believe you threw her at Fasi." Lucas shook his head. "You just picked her up and tossed her."

Draif hopped over the back of the couch and settled in beside him. His dark eyes were wet with tears. "I feel better, Lucas, and my head's clearer. I loved Dottie. I can say that now."

Lucas pulled him into his side. "Good."

"I can't believe you all did that for me," Draif said. "I didn't even know that was what I needed."

"You're my mate," Lucas said. "I'll always do my best to take care of you. The others are your friends and family. We love you."

Draif nuzzled his neck, licking away a drop of sweat. He ran a hand over Lucas's crotch and cupped his dick.

Lucas groaned. "Now?"

"Only if you want to," Draif said, biting down on

Lucas's neck. Lucas's dick hardened fast as Draif stroked him through his pants.

"Love, I always want to," Lucas said and smiled.

The next morning, Draif leaned back in his office chair. His new collection of Druffle explored their tunnels while Chutney and Honey watched them, fascinated. Marmalade ignored everyone while she napped.

"Gus just got ahold of Malone's personal identification number. He's been transferring other people's debt into Malone's name."

Ige chuckled. "They're really feeling the pressure. Even with the support of Rueal and Vextonar, things are starting to crumble. A good third of their fleet here in Rueal disbanded because they haven't been paid in two cycles. From what I hear, the fleet that went to Vextonar is staying strong but only because the Vextonian President is paying them straight from the money they're making from selling their citizens."

"Gus said Malone is acting as the middleman," Draif said. "She wanted to branch into slavery, and this has given her the perfect chance."

"What are we going to do?"

Draif tapped his fingers against the arm of his chair. He had a much better handle on his emotions than he had yesterday, but he still felt a little numb.

"Draif?"

He looked up, shaking his head. "We sent sixteen ships, and Crow picked up more friends. Many who left Rueal when HF took over went to Tammol. They want in on the upcoming attack. He says in another couple of weeks, they'll be ready to go."

"When their factories go, Cortez and Hald will be done," Ige said. "That's where the bulk of their investments are."

Draif nodded. "I wonder what they'll do. If they were acting sensibly, they would dissolve the coalition and rebuild."

"They aren't being sensible," Ige said. "I don't know what is driving them, but it's not just hatred, and it's not just business."

"Draif," Ava said, rushing into the room. "I have wonderful news!"

Ige yelped, and the screen went blank.

"Oh dear. Did I interrupt one of your covert meetings?"

Draif smiled softly. "Yes, but we were finished. What's your wonderful news?"

Ava grinned. "First, the Council has elected a new member to replace Brinanda. Her name is Holli, and she's a friend of my family's. I've known her for years."

"Good. This means they can get back to establishing the Bracken as a species, right?"

"Yes," she said, nodding. "Also, the Drellian Chieftain has agreed to work with us. Your friend Rainer was very helpful. Thank you."

Draif's comm chimed, and he held his wrist up. "Reed?"

"Our mole just asked me to sneak in a small group of *friends*," Reed said. "He also wants me to get you to the Lord Admiral, so they can kill you both at once."

Draif shared a puzzled look with Ava. "Why me?"

Reed smiled sweetly. "As a gift to me for my cooperation."

Ava chuckled. "How kind of him."

———

"Can't we settle this between us?" Draif asked, fully aware of the twelve assassins blending in with the others on the walkway outside of the central command building.

"No," Reed said, snarling. "I insist we bring this to the Lord Admiral's attention. You can't get out of this by batting your pretty eyes."

Draif had to stifle a laugh. *So, Reed likes my eyes, huh?*

"Fine. Let's get this over with."

Draif slowly walked toward the building, Reed following him. He took his time, not wanting any of the assassins to get left behind.

He noticed the assassins split up, three staying outside and the rest following them into the building. They stayed far enough back not to draw Draif's attention but could easily pass as being with Draif and Reed.

Enforcement was non-existent in the hallway. *Thank you, Renee,* Draif thought. None of the office people in the building were curious enough to question them.

Harley and Fergus stood from their desks as Draif pushed into Fasi's waiting area. They weren't supposed to be there. Fasi had given them all today off.

Draif looked around. At least there weren't any cleaning bots in the room. Their mole was being extra cautious.

Harley gave him a concerned look and moved to stand between Reed and Draif. "What's wrong, Captain Ando?"

Fergus looked at his tablet, the Cardinal's ears twitching in irritation. "Neither of you are scheduled for a meeting with the Lord Admiral. He canceled all his appointments today."

"Does he have a minute?" Draif said, sighing. "Reed here is upset with me."

"Captain Ando?" Kaylessa's heels clicked on the hard tile as she walked into the room. Fasi's senior personal assistant frowned at the nine people standing in front of the door. "Who are these people with you?"

Uh oh, Draif thought.

One of the assassins grabbed Kaylessa's arm while another two moved toward Fergus and Harley. The remaining six darted toward Fasi's door.

"I got these," Reed said. "Keep the Lord Admiral safe."

Draif spun around and grabbed one of the assassins, hefting her up and tossing her toward the others. It had worked with Ginger yesterday, and it worked this time.

She landed on three of the assassins, and they fell against Fasi's office door, forcing it open. They were dead before they could pick themselves up. Otto, Bendix, and two more Half Moon assassins were awaiting them.

Draif quickly drew one of his vibroblades and sent it flying toward the closest assassin, skewering him. He hopped over the man and pulled his blade from the body, using it to block an attack from another assassin.

He turned around when Harley screamed.

Fergus was fighting with one of the assassins, and Reed had killed another. The third was about to stab Reed from behind.

Before Draif or Reed could act, Kaylessa yelled and hopped on the assassin's back, smacking the top of his head with her hand.

Draif grinned and drew his phaser, shooting the man in the chest until his shielding failed. He collapsed forward, and Kaylessa landed on him.

Fergus yelped and clutched his arm while Reed finished off the last assassin.

Draif turned back to Fasi's office.

Fasi sat at his desk, paperwork spread out in front of him. He looked a little disappointed.

"I didn't get to do anything." The Lord Admiral pouted.

Bendix sat on his desk and gave him a sympathetic

look. "That's what happens when you go into administration."

Otto nudged a dead body with his boot. "Equinox is worse than I thought they were. You send *one* assassin to do the job. Maybe two if it's a big target. This is just clumsy."

"I know," Bendix said, shaking his head in disappointment. "Quality assassins are hard to find anymore. Look at how they botched up kidnapping Icarus. If I was leading their team, I would have waited until Beck and Beol were sleeping and snuck into the house. Instead, the idiots just barged in and made grabby hands."

Otto went to stand next to the window behind Fasi. "I was sure they would send an assassin through the window here. If I was going to kill Fasi, I would scale the wall, make a small hole in the window since it's reinforced, and shoot him in the back of the head."

Fasi groaned. "Can you two just be thankful Equinox is apparently bad at their job and stop talking about killing me?"

Draif frowned. "There were three more assassins outside."

Fasi's comm chimed, and he read the message, eyes growing dark with anger. "Lucas and Finn followed the assassins. The bastards went to our neighborhood. Moses, Shae, and Renee had all the kids at the park."

Draif shook his head, terror filling him as he thought of the kids. "No."

"Shae kept the kids' attention from the fight with a

song." Fasi swallowed hard. "Thank the gods for that Siren. The kids don't know anything happened."

"The assassins are dead?" Draif barely recognized his own voice.

"Moses burnt one to a crisp, and Lucas and Finn easily killed the other. Renee kept one alive – briefly. He told her they were ordered to kill my grandbabies."

Draif's eyes narrowed, and he spun around. He'd kill the fucking traitorous mole.

Reed grabbed him. "Whoa there, Draif. I know what you're thinking, but we need to keep our mole alive for a few more days."

"A mole?" Kaylessa dusted her skirt off. "Someone is spying on us?"

"Into Fasi's office," Bendix said, gesturing them inside.

Harley helped Fergus in, and Otto checked over the young man's wounds.

"HF has been watching us. They are using listening devices and eavesdropping," Fasi said.

Harley's eyes widened. "It's Gary, isn't it?"

"The janitor?" Kaylessa frowned. "Of course, it's not him."

Draif nudged Harley's shoulder with his own. "It *is* Gary. How did you know?"

She shot Kaylessa a smug look. "He's always lurking around and trying to put more cleaning bots into the office. Plus, he keeps making these creepy comments about the Lord Admiral. I guess he assumes since I'm mostly human I must want a human leader."

Fergus laughed. "You're married to a Grell."

Harley shrugged. "I didn't say the man made sense."

"Alright. This is what happened," Fasi said. "These assassins attacked, and Draif and my personal assistants managed to kill them, but not before I was gravely wounded. Okay?"

Draif turned to the three personal assistants. "Reed will go spread the news to Gary, but you three never saw him. He left me at the door to run to the restroom before our talk with Fasi. Understand?"

They nodded.

"You five shield up again," Draif said, nodding to Bendix and the others. "I'll call medical. Renee's already prepared a team to play along."

Harley bit her lip. "Why exactly can't we go kill Gary now?"

Kaylessa swatted at her. "Harley!"

Harley frowned. "Don't act all offended, Kaylessa. They tried to kill our Lord Admiral and his grandchildren."

Kaylessa looked thoughtful. "Good point. Why can't we go kill him now?"

"We need him to report back to HF," Draif said, looking up from his comm. "The medics are on their way. Renee will be here soon too."

———

NEWLY APPOINTED COUNCILWOMAN HOLLI HAD A VOICE that would carry all the way to the Crellic System. "This has gone far enough. Charybdis Station has a responsibility to its people, not the whole damn galaxy. Look what our meddling has brought us."

"She's right," Councilman Delino said. "The Lord Admiral may not make it through the night, but even if he does, he can't be there for our people. It's time to focus on Charybdis Station, not Humans First."

"I don't like it," Councilwoman Rundel said, sighing. "You're right, but I really don't like it."

"We put plans into place in case something like this happened," Councilwoman Jalina said sadly. "The Council will rule until Fasi is physically able."

"Very well." Councilman Mitchell looked tired. "Am I right in assuming our first course of action will be to focus on expanding our budget instead of worrying about Humans First? War is costly, and this whole botched mess has been a financial drain."

"This isn't right," Cas said, surging to his feet. "My father is close to dying, and you want to back off?"

"I agree with Cas," Sheiria said, standing. "We won't stand by for this."

"You two don't have a choice," Councilman Warren said. "You are *our* generals, and we are the Council."

"My fleet follows me," Cas said, snarling. "We're going to Bredell to offer aid. It's what we should have done as soon as they were attacked."

"The Red Fleet will join you," Sheiria said, shaking her head. "I'm disgusted with the lot of you."

The two generals strode from the room, and Audre and Finn exchanged worried looks.

"Let them leave," Councilwoman Holli said. "They'll be back soon enough. Besides, ever since the Element

Air destroyed their resorts, Bredell has been asking us for help. They're wealthy, and we could use the credits."

Pops raised his hand, looking nervous. "That would just leave The Yellow and Blue Fleets here. Remember that several of General Shepard's ships are down for repairs. Is that enough to defend Charybdis?"

Councilman Delino snorted. "Obviously, Humans First isn't coming here themselves. We'll increase the security at the spaceport to keep out assassins."

"It's settled then," Councilwoman Jalina said and waved Draif over. "Captain Ando, will you go fetch Kaylessa? We have quite a bit of paperwork to fill out."

"Yes, Councilwoman." He dipped his head, then slipped out the door, startling the janitor Gary.

The human bowed his head, avoiding Draif's eyes. "Sorry, Captain Ando."

Draif gave him a sad look. "My fault, Gary. It's been a rough day for everyone."

"Yes," the man agreed, then went back to checking over the cleaning bot in front of him.

Draif sent Kaylessa in, then headed home. He desperately wanted to check on the kids. The assassins hadn't even gotten close, but still.

Moses sat on the front porch, weathered face tilted up.

Draif sat beside him. "The kids are okay, right?"

"Yes," Moses said, patting Draif's knee. "You know I'll protect my tribe, boy. I may be old, but I still know a few tricks."

"I'm sorry. I can't help but worry. I promised Leti I

would watch out for them, and then I didn't even think of someone trying to hurt them."

"Sometimes it's hard to remember people can be so cruel," Moses said. "They wanted to kill Fasi's grandchildren because they know he loves them. There's nothing more than hatred behind an idea like that."

Bendix suddenly appeared beside him, shield dissolving. He sat on Draif's other side. "The neighborhood is clear of Gary's cleaning bots."

Draif pulled his knees up beneath his chin. "Bendix, how much would it cost to send some of Half Moon—"

"Don't ask that unless you mean it," Bendix interrupted Draif. "Guild Master Beol and I have talked a lot about integrating the guild into Charybdis Station. That means any contract we complete for you will be for Charybdis Station."

"HF will attack Charybdis Station sooner or later," Moses said. "Their leaders, though, will direct their fleets from their cushy offices. It's not right."

"Plus, no matter how many hired ships Charybdis takes down, Humans First will just buy more when they're able and send them," Bendix added.

"Your guild offers the station a whole new fighting strategy, and we would be stupid not to utilize it," Draif said.

"If the Lord Admiral approves it, I'll move people into place," Bendix said. "Don't just focus on the big four. If someone can easily take over their position, then you've slowed them down instead of defeating them."

Draif nodded. "I'll talk to Fasi."

"Let me know what he decides." Bendix stood. "I'm keeping a few of my people in your neighborhood just in case. Your mole is less likely to use Reed now that he thinks the captain may be on your radar for staging the assassination attempt."

"We'll be picking him up next week," Draif said. "Once he reports to HF that Charybdis Station is vulnerable, he'll be arrested and confined."

"Good." Bendix waved, then activated his shield, disappearing.

"I wonder if he ever spies on people when he's shielded," Moses said, rubbing his chin.

"Hey, I can respect people's privacy." Bendix's voice came from a few feet away. "Mostly."

1 4

Lucas watched Sami and Pepper jump up and down on the big bed in Leti and Hack's room. The Lord Admiral watched them carefully, ready to catch one if they fell. Pax and Aagy did the same from the floor.

"I can't believe they sent assassins after the kids," he whispered. His ears lay flat, and his tail twitched.

Renee's face twisted with anger before she took a deep breath and forced it away. "The fuckers are dead, and it won't be long before their clients are too."

Lucas rubbed his face. "They got close. I swear my tail's going to turn gray. I really need a catnip day."

Renee chuckled. "You can have a catnip week once we've handled Humans First."

Lucas smiled. "We all need a break."

"We do. I think my mate will enjoy staying here for a week," Renee said wryly.

Rizzie pushed open the bedroom door with her

butt and dragged her tea party table into the room. "It's tea party time, Grandpa."

"Perfect," Fasi said, smiling fondly at his granddaughter. "Milo should be ready for lunch too. Rosie girl, would you go get him?"

Rose smiled and stood from her chair. "Sure, Grandpa."

Mo moved from his own seat and helped Rizzie set up her table.

"Oh yeah," Lucas said. "Fasi will be just fine staying in the bedroom for a week. You'll keep the kids home too, right?"

"Yes," Renee said. "Everyone thinks he's been gravely injured, so their instructors are more than understanding."

"I'm surprised people aren't rushing over to check on you all," Lucas said.

"Finn and Audre are working with Enforcement to stop people at the tram. They're telling them to come back next week."

Draif came in and started counting heads. "Where's Rosie, Alex, and Milo?"

"Milo and I are right here," Rose said from the door, Milo in her arms. "Alex just went to sit down with Grandpa Moses. I think they want to guard the house."

Lucas pulled Draif into his arms. "Everyone is safe, love."

Draif shuddered, then sank against him. "We weren't expecting them to come here."

"I'm glad we were there," Lucas said. "Honestly,

Moses would probably have taken them out even if we weren't there. These kids are well protected."

"Alex wants to move back in now," Renee said. "That young man needs to spread his wings, not worry about his family."

Lucas felt his comm buzz with a message. He held his wrist up and read it. "It looks like Dottie's son just arrived at the spaceport. I asked one of my buddies to keep an eye out for him."

Draif buried his face against Lucas's chest. "I don't want to go."

"Yes, you do." Lucas stroked his fingers through Draif's hair. He knew Draif would hate himself if he didn't go to greet Abe. His mate was probably the most responsible person Lucas had ever met.

"Alright. I meant I don't *want* to have to do this."

Renee patted Draif's back. "It's best to get it over with, dear. Pops is bringing you more Druffle in the morning, and Ma will be at your house later tonight. They didn't join in our sparring, so they want to comfort you in their own way."

"That means hugs and kisses, Uncle Draify," Rizzie said, running over to hug Draif. "I'm sorry your friend died. We'll remember her together, okay? You can tell me stories about her, then I'll know her too."

Draif kissed the top of her head. "Thanks, Rizzie. Dottie was a good person. I'll tell you all about her, but first, I need to go talk to her son."

The little Siren squeezed him tightly for a moment longer, then ran back to her table. "Stop jumping on the bed! It's tea time."

Lucas pulled Draif to the door. "Run, before she makes us sit in the tiny chairs."

They left quickly, passing Moses and Alex on the way. The two men both watched the neighborhood with sharp eyes.

"What the hell is this?" Lucas asked, pulling up short at the tram.

The shuttle tram platform was full of Charybdis Station citizens, all wearing worried expressions. Enforcement kept them from entering the neighborhood, but Lucas could tell the visitors were frightened.

"Damn it," Draif said, quietly. "I didn't think about how the public would react."

"I don't think anyone did," Lucas said. "If they had, the Council would have made an announcement right away. We don't want our people panicking."

Draif stepped up to the front of the crowd and held his hands up. "Can I have your attention for a moment?"

The sea of people quieted down.

Lucas smiled happily, tail swishing. His mate loved taking charge and looked damn good doing it.

"I know many of you, but not everyone. I'm Captain Draif Ando of the Blue Fleet. I'm a close friend of the Lord Admiral's family. I know you're all concerned for him and for the station. The Council will release a formal statement soon, but they are stepping up to ensure the station runs smoothly until our Lord Admiral is able to return to his position."

"He will return, won't he?" The Grell asking the question had a dish of food in his hands.

"Yes," Draif said firmly.

"Are Renee and his grandkids alright?" The woman carried a dish of food too.

"They're as well as can be expected," Draif said. "I see many of you have food and other thoughtful gifts. Please leave them here, and I'll have someone come get them. I know Renee and the kids will appreciate your generosity, but they need privacy right now. I, for one, plan on sharing that delicious-looking casserole with Rizzie. She loves potatoes."

The man carrying the casserole grinned proudly. "It's my family's recipe."

Draif smiled softly and nodded. "We'll make sure to update everyone soon. If you have any questions or concerns, please don't hesitate to message me. I'll do my best to help."

People started handing the enforcement officers their gifts and piling back onto the tram. Lucas messaged Alex, telling him to send someone to pick up what the crowd had left. He noted each person looked relieved.

Draif made his way back to Lucas.

Lucas tilted the shorter man's face up and gently kissed him. "Have I told you lately how much I love you?"

Draif chuckled. "Yeah. This morning when I fed Wobble that carrot you didn't want to eat."

"Carrots are disgusting. As many wonderful things

as the Human Diaspora gave us, the carrot isn't one of them."

Draif snorted. "Let's go before we miss Abe."

Lucas followed him. "What you did back there was exactly what was needed. That's the thing about you, Draif. You always step up and do the job. I don't just love you; I respect you. I'm proud to be your lieutenant."

Draif cupped his face and stood on his tiptoes to give him a kiss. "The only reason I can do half of what I do is because you support me. I feel corny saying it, but you're my rock. I know you'll always be there. Even before I knew I loved you, I knew that."

A man jostled them, then apologized before moving on.

"We have somewhere to be," Lucas said, pleasure filling him at Draif's words. That night, though, there *would* be a massive amount of cuddling.

They got on the shuttle tram and made it to the spaceport within minutes.

Lucas held Draif's hand as they walked to the correct dock. "Don't think I didn't notice you somehow managed not to lie to anyone."

Draif squeezed his hand. "I didn't realize so many people would be upset by this, and I should have."

"This wasn't something you could control, Draif. Sometimes shit happens, and we just have to deal with it."

Draif gave him a disgruntled look. "I like having control."

Lucas grinned slowly. "I like it when you have control."

"I bet you do." Bendix's voice came from the empty space behind them, startling Lucas.

"Why are you following us?" Draif asked.

"The Lord Admiral ordered me to. He said you were a target earlier too, so someone needed to keep a guard on you."

"Why are you shielded then?" Draif asked.

"So I can hear all the good stuff. Now, Lucas, what does Draif use to tie you down before a scene?"

Lucas started laughing.

They reached Abe's ship before he could reply, but Lucas knew by Draif's glower, both Lucas and Bendix would get an earful when they got back home.

Dottie's son was helping an elderly hybrid from the ship when they arrived. People stood among neatly stacked crates, some clearly family and others alone. All looked tired and emotionally drained.

Abe left the woman with a group and came to Draif, surprising Lucas's mate with a hug. "It's a pleasure to finally meet you."

Draif stiffly hugged the man back. "I'm so sorry I couldn't save Dottie."

Abe snorted. "Mom didn't want saving, Draif. She wanted to help every last person she could before the monsters caught her."

Draif opened his mouth to reply, but just sighed. "You're right. She was so damn stubborn."

Abe patted his shoulder. "She sent some things for you."

"She told me she would," Draif said, shuffling his feet.

Lucas stepped forward. "Hi. I'm Draif's mate, Lucas. We'll get a couple of shuttles and help you all get situated. The Lord Admiral set aside living space for Vextonar's refugees."

"I heard he was hurt," Abe said, looking concerned. "HF sent assassins after him."

Lucas struggled to find the right words. Subterfuge wasn't his forte.

"Ask us for details next week," Draif said simply.

Abe gave him a curious look, then shrugged. "Okay. You know, you kind of remind me of Mom. She would give you a hint of something, but nothing incriminating."

Lucas had never seen Draif smile so brightly. "I'll consider that a compliment," Draif said.

Abe laughed. "Alright. Now, your packages."

He handed Draif a small data cube from his pocket. "Mom said to give this to you. I have no idea what's on it, but she wanted you to have it."

"Thanks," Draif said. "I'll look at it as soon as I get home."

"Mom said only you would know the security password. She said it was something she mentioned to you during one of your calls."

Draif frowned. "I'll have to think on it. I appreciate you giving this to me. We should get you all moved into your new homes."

"That wasn't all Mom sent you." Abe looked nervous, then turned and waved at one of the people helping passengers from the ship. "I'm not sure how welcome your other packages will be, but Mom was insistent."

The man at the ship ducked inside, and a moment later, he led five people and a dog from the ship. They were clearly a Wello-hybrid family. The father was close to fifty years old, and the mother was in her late forties. Their children looked to be around twenty, fifteen, and twelve years old.

The man froze when he saw Draif, his face draining of all color. "Oh gods, you look just like your mother."

Draif frowned. "How do you know that?"

Lucas thought of Draif's past and quickly did the math. "You're Draif's father?"

———

Lucas opened the front door of their home and set the bags he carried at the bottom of the staircase. The Depray family didn't have much with them, but it was more than some.

He turned to Leander and his family. "Why don't we sit in the living room and talk?"

Draif hadn't said anything since he met his father. He seemed to be in shock. Lucas had decided the middle of a spaceport wasn't the right place for a conversation like this and led them all back to Lucas and Draif's home.

"Thank you," Leander said and set down his own bags.

Draif's eldest half-sibling, Tempest, shuffled her

feet. "Do you want me, Innis, and Chay to bring the bags somewhere?"

Lucas smiled. "Good idea. There are three empty bedrooms upstairs if you would like to decide who goes where."

Leander's wife, Sybil, pushed Draif's father toward the living room. "We'll be right here if you need us, kids."

Tempest nodded and grabbed as many bags as she could carry before leading her two younger brothers upstairs.

Bonbon, their fuzzy brown and white Vexal dog, followed them.

Lucas looked at Draif. His mate stood in the entryway, eyes glazed.

"Come on, love. Talk to me."

Draif blinked. "That's my father."

Lucas cupped Draif's face, thumbs caressing his cheeks. "You said he tried to buy you and your mom."

Marmalade padded down the stairs, going straight to Draif. Lucas had noticed she always knew when his mate was upset.

Draif picked the chubby cat up and held her to his chest. "Mom's master wouldn't sell her, and Leander couldn't afford me."

"Do you want them here?" Lucas winced. "I kind of took over when I invited them."

"Now Bendix will want to know what you tie *me* up with," Draif said, eyes still unfocused.

"He's not wrong." Bendix's voice came from the empty space beside them.

"Do you really need to be here?" Lucas asked.

"Guard duty, so yeah."

"Draif?" Leander came to stand beside them. "We don't have to do this if you don't want to. Sybil and I can take the kids and go."

Draif glared at Leander and stomped his foot. "No. You're not leaving again."

Leander's eyes watered. "I didn't want to leave the first time."

"To the living room," Lucas said and gently nudged the two men into the room.

"Oh, Draif," Sybil said. "Your father truly didn't want to leave you or your mother with that man. He saved his money for years, hoping to buy you."

"That asshole wouldn't even think of selling Gretchen, but he told me he'd sell you for two hundred and fifty thousand credits," Leander said. "No one would loan me the money, but Sybil and I both saved every credit we could."

"By the time we had the money, you had already been sold," Sybil said, voice breaking. "We talked to Mr. Ando, but he increased the price."

"I was with Leti then," Draif said, voice soft. "I was okay. Leti's my brother and my best friend."

"Dottie told us about him," Leander said. "She said she kept an eye on you too."

Sybil looked around the room. "You and your mate have a nice home, and Abe said you were a Charybdis Station captain. You've done well."

Leander's sniffled. "I know it doesn't matter to you, but I'm proud of you, Draif."

Draif's expression grew dark. "Why did you leave?"

Lucas wrapped an arm around Draif's shoulder, pulling his mate close.

Leander closed his eyes, face pained. "Your owner didn't want me near your mother. He made threats, so I left. I've regretted it every day."

"You got married and had a family," Draif said, voice hollow. "You moved on."

"He did marry me and have a family, Draif," Sybil said. "But he never moved on from losing you. Do you know how hard it was to save three hundred and sixty thousand credits on our salaries? Lord Ando demanded four hundred thousand, and we were almost there when you and your friend left Vextonar. Both of us worked as many jobs as we could, hoping to bring you home."

"Tempest did too," Leander said quietly. "When she turned eighteen, she got a housekeeping job with a Prime family. She put anything extra she made into the Draif fund. Even Innis and Chay added what credits they made doing odd jobs around the neighborhood."

"The Draif fund," Lucas repeated. He leaned over and kissed Draif's head. "You have a fund, love."

Draif's wet eyes moved to Sybil. "I can understand why he would want me, but why did you help him?"

The woman raised her arms as if to hold Draif, then quickly lowered them. "Leander's my life mate, but he cared a great deal for your mother, and he loves you. That means I love you. That's how it works."

"It never bothered you?" Lucas asked, a little skeptical.

Sybil snorted. "My life mate loved another woman before he met me. Of course that bothered me. Draif existing? That was a gift, not an annoyance."

"I tried to hide the Draif fund from her at first," Leander said. "I didn't think she would want to spend so much on my son."

"Stupid man," Sybil said, rolling her eyes. "It was hard making a living on Vextonar since we were in the Lower caste, but we managed. We worked hard and saved every credit we could."

"You should have stayed in contact with me," Draif said, voice hoarse. "It would have made a difference."

Leander's face was full of pain. "I'm so sorry, Draif."

Lucas felt a surge of pride when Draif straightened up and nodded. "You're here now. You all will stay here until we find a place close by. If you will give me a third of your savings, I'll invest it. That will get it to work making money for you while we find you work here on Charybdis."

"My house is still empty, love," Lucas said. "I think, by now, you know I'm not leaving."

Draif laughed, voice cracking. "You better not."

"Draify loo? Are you home?" Ma's voice came from the front door.

"In the living room," Lucas called out.

Ma carried a stack of pans and platters filled with food, and Lucas jumped up to help her with them.

She paused as she took in the sight of the remaining bags at the bottom of the stairs and the couple on the couch. "Who are your guests?"

"This is my father, Leander Depray, and his wife, Sybil."

Lucas just barely caught the dishes as Ma released them and ran into the room.

Ma propped her hands on her hips. "Your father? Is this good or bad, Draify loo? They're small. If you want them gone, I can take care of it."

Draif hugged the large Grell, startling her. "I love you Ma. This is a good thing. It's also a hard thing."

She squeezed Draif tightly, picking him up off his feet. "I see. It's an aching good."

"They'll be moving into my house," Lucas said, smiling.

Ma set Draif on his feet. "It'll need a good cleaning, I'm sure. Have you even seen the place?"

Lucas shrugged. "Never needed to."

"How much are you willing to sell it for?" Leander asked. "We have the Draif fund, and since he's no longer a slave, we could spend it on a house."

Sybil eyes grew wide. "Imagine us owning a home, Leander. One right down the road from your Draif."

"Oh, sweetie," Ma said and pulled Sybil off the couch and into a hug. "We're going to be friends. I just know it."

Lucas grinned. "The house was a gift to me from our Lord Admiral. It only seems right I pass that gift along to my mate's family. You won't be paying for it."

Leander shook his head. "That's not right. I wronged Draif and shouldn't be rewarded for it. Besides, you'll be building your own family and need to think of the future."

Lucas hid a smirk. He knew what Draif would say before he even opened his mouth.

"You didn't *wrong* me, Leander. I'm not really angry with you, just the situation. There weren't any good options. Yes, I wish you could have stayed in contact with me, but it would have put yourself and your family at risk."

Leander's eyes watered. "That doesn't mean you should give me a free house."

"My Draify loo has plenty of credits." Ma finally put Sybil back on her feet. "He has a good eye for investing, and my boys know the importance of family. Poor Lucas's parents died almost ten years ago. He could use more family nearby."

Lucas choked on a laugh. Ma and the others had taken him in wholeheartedly. He couldn't walk a hundred feet without coming into contact with his *family*.

Draif sighed sadly and rubbed Lucas's arm. "Yes. Poor Lucas needs you both. Please say you'll accept his gift?" He turned his dark, sad eyes on Leander and Sybil. "Please?"

Leander melted. "Of course. Anything you two need from me is yours."

"Dad!" Chay ran into the room. The youngest Depray was a tiny thing. "Bonbon fell in love with a gray cat upstairs, and Draif has a dragon. She's sitting on Bonbon's head."

15

*L*ucas leaned against the cushioned headboard of their bed, and Draif sat between his legs, back to Lucas's chest, trying different words and phrases to unlock Dottie's data cube.

"How are you feeling about all this?" Lucas asked.

Draif paused for a second, before typing another word in. "I don't know. I've always done my best to not think of my father. He couldn't buy me, and he couldn't stay. I knew that. I really did."

"You wanted him to stay."

"When I was a kid, I wanted him to sweep in and save me. By the time I was ten, I knew that couldn't happen – there was no way. So, I left it behind and focused on my reality. That's been my life ever since. Until I came here."

"You didn't have any hopes and dreams?" Lucas treasured every conversation Draif and he had, but now that he thought about it, the only thing Draif seemed to want from the future was financial security.

"No dreams or hopes that didn't include protecting Leti. I wanted to learn how to fight to protect him. I wanted to learn diplomacy and strategy so I could talk our way out of problems. I wanted to learn business and investing so I could help him stand on his own."

"What about now? You aren't a slave and Leti has Hack."

Draif leaned his head back and kissed Lucas's chin. "Now, all I dream about is keeping everyone safe. Don't get me wrong; I love you and all our friends, but having people to love means I have more to lose. It's scary."

"People die, Draif. That's part of life."

Draif shifted around so he could see Lucas's face. "We don't talk a lot about it, but do you miss your parents?"

Lucas dipped his head and pressed a kiss to Draif's lips. "Yes. I don't think on them too much anymore, but anytime I do, there's a sharp pain in my heart. I think about what Dad would say to me being a lieutenant. He wanted me to go to a big university and be a doctor or something equally impressive. Then I wonder if Mom would complain because I don't have kids yet. I know she would like you though. *That* I don't have to think too hard on."

"I think your dad and mom would both be proud of you. How could they not? You're… you. You work hard and care about people. You're patient and sweet. You don't have an ego the size of the station, even though you should. You're just Lucas. I can't think of any other way to say it."

Lucas grinned. "I'm glad you don't know my flaws yet."

"You snore and steal the covers. You always skip out on your turn to clean the commons, and Ned ends up doing it. You like to gossip and poke your nose into everyone else's business. Also, let's not forget, you buy exotic pets without thinking about who will take care of them."

Lucas gasped. "Chutney practically takes care of Honey for us."

Hearing her name, Honey looked at them from where she was perched on top of one of the bedposts. Chutney had somehow managed to fit on top of another, while Marmalade hadn't even tried. Draif's cat was sleeping at the foot of the bed.

"Yes, well, Chutney may be getting married soon." Draif gestured to the side of the bed. Bonbon lay on the floor, watching Chutney lovingly.

Lucas chuckled. "Okay. Maybe you're right."

"Black herons," Draif said suddenly.

Lucas gave Draif a puzzled look. "Huh?"

"Dottie said I reminded her of a black heron. All this talk of animals made me remember that." Draif typed it into his tablet, and the data cube lit up.

Dottie's face projected above the small square disk. *"Hey kiddo. If you're getting this, then I probably didn't make it off Vextonar."*

"Oh, Dottie," Draif said, eyes filling with tears.

"There are a few things I want to tell you. First, I've included information on the rest of my contacts of the shady

variety. These are people who can get you any information you want for the right price. They're good folks. They just have a stretchy moral code."

A list of names and contact information loaded to Draif's tablet.

"That's a lot of people," Lucas said, eyes widening.

Draif nodded. "Dottie knew everyone. Even if they never made it to Vextonar, she would seek them out."

"Now that's out of the way, it's time I told you something that's been weighing heavy on my mind for years. I've been meaning to tell you for a long time, but it hurts so damn much. Kiddo, your mom was a good friend of mine. She traveled often with that asshole Prime that owned her, and I met her on one of their trips."

Draif's eyes watered. "She never said anything about my mother."

"Gretchen was a good person, Draif. She was beautiful on the outside, but she was so much more than that. She had a mind like a trap and a will made of pure thitetium. She was born into a caste she could never escape, but she was more than some rich Prime's bed-slave. Just like you are more than the son of a bed-slave. More than Leti's best friend. More than a captain of Charybdis Station."

Lucas swallowed hard, blinking away tears. She knew his mate well.

"I was there the first time Gretchen held you in her arms. It took a damn miracle to get into the house and then her room, but I did it. Draif, I wish you could remember the look on her face. She fell in love with you in an instant. She cared for your father, but you, kiddo, you were the love of her life."

Dottie's bright smile dimmed, and her eyes filled with pain.

"When you were a couple of years old, I finally worked my way into a higher position at the spaceport. I finally had the resources to get you both off Vextonar. My plan... My plan failed. Gretchen was caught, and her master killed her. I thank the gods every day you don't remember it. You were too young, but I remember seeing the blood everywhere."

Draif was stiff in Lucas's arms. He stroked a hand through Draif's hair and hugged him tightly.

"After that, I shut down for a while. I couldn't bear to see you, knowing I had failed you both so horribly. Then, one day, this boy struts into my spaceship to pick up a package for his master. I became your friend, and I love you as much as I did your mother.

"I wish I had told you sooner. There are so many stories I could tell you about her. I've written down a lot of my memories of her and included all the pictures I have. It's not enough. I should have been stronger, and for that, I am so sorry."

Files started downloading on Draif's tablet, and one picture caught Lucas's eye. A beautiful brown-skinned woman with wild black hair grinned up at him. The dark rosettes of the Wello species lined the sides of her face, and her black eyes danced with mischief and intelligence.

"She looks just like you," Lucas whispered.

"As far as your father goes, I only met him once or twice. It was Leti that really brought him to my attention. I know Leti offered to find your father many times while you lived on Vextonar. Leti told me you refused each time.

"That doesn't mean that Leti didn't find him anyway. Leti hired an investigator to keep track of him because he wanted to have the information ready just in case you decided you wanted to know more. When this latest shitstorm of the Primes started, Leti asked me to arrange for your father and his family to go to Charybdis Station.

"I couldn't save Gretchen, but I'm glad I was able to help you and Leti. I'm glad I was able to help your father. I hope you can forgive me."

Draif's body shook with his sob.

"I love you, Draif, as much as I do my own Lacey and Abe. I'm proud of the man you've become, and I wish I could be there to see you take on the galaxy. You'll do amazing things, Draif Ando, and I don't just mean take down Humans First. You're my black heron, and you'll have the galaxy at your feet in no time."

Dottie's face disappeared, and Draif dropped the tablet, turning around to bury his face against Lucas's neck.

Lucas wiped away his own tears and held his mate as he cried.

After a while, Draif's tears slowed and silence filled the room.

"Your mom was murdered," Lucas said.

"By Harrison Goel."

"What? Goel was your former master?"

"I didn't want anyone to know. I was afraid they would think I was using this for revenge or something. That's how Beldon first saw me. Cortez is Goel's neighbor. Apparently, he had his eye on me for a while before I was sold to the compound."

"Draif, I can almost guarantee no one would have thought badly of you."

"He's right." Bendix's voice came from the open door.

Honey hissed and let out a tiny stream of fire.

"Bendix!" Lucas scowled. "What the fuck, man?"

"The door was open. If you wanted privacy, you should have shut it." The bed shifted as Bendix sat. "Anyway, I doubt anyone would have thought you were making things up just for revenge. Fuck, you have enough money to order a hit on the man yourself."

Draif wiped his nose on his sleeve. "It's not important to the mission. I'm glad he'll die, but he didn't just murder my mother. He's done so much worse."

"That doesn't mean I don't envy Doris," Bendix said grumpily. "She's the one assigned to Goel."

"I'll send her some names," Draif said. "Most of the servants and slaves are probably still there. Cook would love to see Goel die. She hates him almost as much as me."

"Why?" Lucas asked.

"Goel liked the looks of her daughter. He made her his bed-slave, then traded her off to a friend when he got tired of her. Cook can't contact her at all."

"Fuck slavery," Bendix said.

Lucas could hear the snarl in his voice even if he couldn't see it. "We can talk to Fasi in the morning. It's a good idea to let him know, just in case it comes up."

"Okay," Draif said, looking drained. "Bendix, go stalk someone else. It's bedtime."

"I want to see what kind of bindings you two use."

"Out!" Lucas pointed at the door, trying not to laugh.

"You two are no fun."

16

A week later, Draif smiled and waved at Gary the janitor as Enforcement carried him away. Pops and Lucas stood on either side of him.

"Alright, folks," Pops said, waving to the group of engineers behind him. "Collect all the cleaning bots and let's start tearing them apart."

"I can't wait to watch this station burn," Gary yelled, struggling against the Enforcement officers. "You'll all hurt, just like your filthy Lord Admiral."

"Hi, Gary," Fasi said, walking past the struggling man.

Draif ignored Gary's loud curses and focused on Fasi. "I bet there are a lot of people happy to see you out of the house."

"Why do you think I'm late? Everyone kept stopping me."

"It's your own fault, Lord Admiral," Councilwoman Holli said. "You've made our people love you."

The remaining Enforcement officers finished

sweeping the conference room and left while everyone took their seats.

"Alright," Fasi said. "I've enjoyed the vacation, but it's time to get back to work. Sheiria is about a third of the way to Beton, and Cas is two weeks from Tammol. They'll start working with the other forces to plan their attacks."

"Hack is about a week from Genarg," Finn said. "The scouts there have eyes on the Queen and Earth. They aren't doing much, but at least they're on the planet."

Fasi looked around the table. "Bendix and Draif have asked my permission to put Half Moon assassins in place to kill Humans First's leadership."

Draif leaned back, watching the Council's discussion. It would happen even if he had to pay another assassin guild himself.

"It won't look good that we hire an assassin to solve our problems," Councilwoman Jalina said. "We're just asking for retaliation."

"It does set a bad precedent," Councilman Mitchell added.

"What if we weren't sending assassins?" Fasi said thoughtfully. "What if we were sending covert operatives?"

"We aren't technically at war with Humans First," Councilwoman Rundell said. "We've tried to stay off their radar so far. Not that we're any good at that."

"When they attack us, and they will, we will be at war with them." Fasi said.

The Council members looked at one another,

clearly uncomfortable with the idea of using Half Moon.

Draif leaned forward. "How about this? You all vote to make Half Moon its own division within Charybdis, and Bendix puts his people in place. When Humans First attacks, we declare war and give Bendix the go ahead."

Councilman Delino grinned. "I like the way you think. Bendix can go ahead and put his people in place while we do the paperwork. The timing needs to be just right. If their leadership is taken out during their attack, you can bet that will hobble them. It doesn't matter that the big four are in other systems. They're the ones paying the salaries and giving the orders."

"That I can stand behind," Councilwoman Jalina added, nodding. "Bendix, will your Guild Master agree to it?"

"Yeah. We've already talked about the ways he is willing to integrate with Charybdis Station. I'll have a chat with him tonight, but I'm sending Half Moon out tomorrow morning. This is our home too, and we *will* protect it." He looked at Draif. "Goel and the others *will* die by our hands no matter what you decide."

Fasi nodded, snarling. "I understand and fully support that statement. Everyone, let's figure out how to make this shit work."

———

LATER THAT DAY, DRAIF WATCHED HIS CREW SPAR IN THE Blue Fleet's training compound. The other crews had been surprised to see them there, and Draif knew they watched him closely, curious about the bed-slave turned captain.

Reed brought his crew to the mats beside them and nodded at Draif. "Ignore the stares, Draif. They'll get used to you soon enough."

Draif gave him a half-smile, then tried to focus on his crew. Anders and Crimson worked together against Ned and Alex. Normally, he would watch them closely and call out suggestions, but Draif's skin itched all over, and his mind couldn't seem to concentrate.

All those months of planning, and now that events were progressing, life decided to get complicated. Draif understood people—their motives and behavior could be deciphered with a little researching and contemplation. When it came to his own feelings though, he was useless.

The only thing he was certain of was that he loved Lucas with every shred of his being. As for his father, stepmom, and stepsiblings? He was tangled mess of pain, jealousy, and aching love.

They had tried to help him, and for that, he was appreciative, but Sybil and her children hadn't been sold to a bed-slave training compound. They hadn't been sexually abused, then permanently maimed.

His thoughts on Dottie and her secrets weren't any easier to understand. He wished she would have told him about his mother before. There had been a time he would have killed for a picture of the woman.

At the same time though, his heart swelled at the

thought that Dottie had loved him. She had seen more in him than any other person except Leti.

Oh, Leti. He had asked Dottie to help Draif's father without knowing anything about the man. Draif didn't know what to think. Should he be mad Leti made that decision? Should he be happy his family was safe? Honestly, he felt a little of both.

It had been a week since he'd spoken to his best friend, his brother. He knew Leti was starting to get frustrated that Draif kept avoiding his calls and ignoring his messages, but he didn't know what to say yet.

A blast of fire scalded the wall above Draif's head, and Draif jumped.

"Captain, why aren't you paying attention to us?" Alex and the others lined up in front of him, all looking concerned.

"You haven't said anything about my kicks," Ned said, hands on his hips.

Draif laughed hard. "I'm sorry. My head isn't where it needs to be. Anders, will you take over?"

The large man nodded. "Sure thing, Captain. Maybe you should hunt down Lucas? He was going to the engineering district with Tae."

Draif could certainly use Lucas right now, but he didn't want to pull his mate away from work every time he felt upset. He'd deal with this on his own.

"Uh, Draif. I mean, Captain Ando." Finn strode across the Blue Sector's training room.

Draif hid a smile and saluted. "Blue Lieutenant. How can I help you?"

Finn's ears twitched, and he looked extremely guilty. "General Hackett ordered me to sit you down to talk with Leti. He doesn't like it when his mate gets upset."

Draif groaned. "Damn it. I need some time."

"I'm so sorry." Finn turned his tablet around. Leti's green eyes glared at him from the screen.

"What the peanut butter fudge, Draif? I've called you a million times!"

Draif rolled his eyes. "You only called thirty-four times."

"Why didn't you answer?"

Draif rubbed his hands through his hair. "My father arrived a week ago."

Leti squeaked, his hands going to his cheeks. "What is he like? Is he a selfish, cowardly jerk or is he a tragically misunderstood older version of you?"

A hoarse laugh escaped him. "He's neither. He's just a man with a family."

"He really did move on?" Leti's lip trembled, and his eyes watered.

"No. He found his life mate, and they worked together to save money. They wanted to buy me, Leti. They had a Draif fund."

Leti wiggled in place, then spun around, squealing. "He's a good man! Oh, Draif. That means you have another father. I need to check with Pops and Fasi to make sure they know you still love them. You know how they get."

"Pops and Fasi are *your* fathers, Leti. Not mine."

Leti's eyebrows rose. "I'm telling them you said that."

The screen went blank.

"Damn it." Draif scowled at Finn. "That wasn't how I wanted that conversation to go."

Finn shrugged and tucked his tablet under his arm. "Yet, here we are. At least it's over. Don't think I didn't notice you've been on edge this week."

Draif sighed, then turned back to his crew. The four men stood there watching him.

"Back to work! Anders, you know better than to let your guard down when Crimson's on the ground. Just because he's down, doesn't mean he's out of the fight. Ned, I swear to the gods, your legs aren't noodles, so put some power behind those kicks. Alex, if you shoot fire at me again, I'll put you on cleaning duty for the next year."

The men whooped as they went back to the mats, and Draif lost himself in training for another hour.

Then they came.

Fasi, Pops, and Leander made an interesting picture as they strode across the training room. The two hulking Grell and the tiny Wello man all wore identical disgruntled expressions.

The other soldiers and captains of the Blue Fleet stopped training and watched the Lord Admiral, faces curious.

"Draif." Fasi practically growled his name. "Explain to me why Leti told me you think Pops and I aren't your fathers?"

Draif groaned. "Because you two *aren't* my fathers. I get that you've adopted Leti, but I'm not Leti."

"No, you're not," Fasi said, confused. "You're Draif – a tenacious and skilled man with an underdeveloped sense of worth."

"You're our Draify loo," Pops said, shaking his head. "We love you, and you're our son as much as you are Leander's."

"It's true, Draif," Leander said. "These two men have spent the past week telling me about all your accomplishments and how proud they are of you. They've also told me how they've worried about you settling in and adjusting to life as a free man. We are all three your fathers, young man!"

Draif struggled to find something to say, eyes blinking away tears. He thought about what Dottie had told him. *You'll do amazing things.*

"Okay." Draif swallowed hard. "You're my fathers. Now, go away. People are staring."

————

"Then they all hugged you? Right there in the Blue Fleet training room?" Lucas started laughing.

Draif groaned. "Stop laughing. It was so embarrassing. Finn even called Leti on his tablet, so he saw the whole thing."

Lucas laughed harder.

Draif reached around and pulled Lucas's tail. "You're lucky I love you."

Lucas picked him up and spun him around. "Yes. I am."

"Uh, am I interrupting something?" Gus stood in the doorway of Draif's office. "Tempest let me in. She's downstairs cooking dinner."

Draif grabbed Lucas's ears and squeezed them. "Come in, Gus. My mate is putting me down now. Then, I'm going to sit on his lap while you and I talk about Charybdis Station's defenses."

Lucas didn't set him down. He just sat and settled Draif into his lap.

Draif shrugged. That worked too.

Gus grinned. "So is this how all the captains and their lieutenants act?"

few days later, Draif sat in his office. He watched the video Rainer had sent him, horrified. "That's the Queen. She's supposed to be on Genarg."

Rainer shook his head and waved his hands. "This is from this morning. She left the planet completely ruined three hours after landing. I don't understand. Why would they hide her away? Your scouts sent video of her on Genarg. They saw her in person."

Draif quickly sent a message to Finn. Hack needed to know they were flying into a trap.

In the video, the Queen stood in one of the open-air spaceports of Port Broacia, a planet in the Radiant System. She held her hands up and wind whipped around her, quickly building into several huge cyclones. They flew from her and began tearing into everything in their path.

The Queen's laugh was frighteningly joyful as she

stomped one foot. The ground rumbled, and the earth began to move.

Draif couldn't turn away from the video. The human holding it laughed as he spun around, trying to catch as much of the devastation as possible. "Survivors?"

"Some," Rainer said, voice soft. "My Chieftain ordered ships to search the planet for more. Drell and Eloide are the only habitable planets left in the Radiant System that Humans First hasn't destroyed."

Draif trembled as he watched people scream as buildings fell into fissures or were torn apart by the growing storm.

He fumbled as he pulled a screen up to call Crow.

The man's face appeared quickly. "Draif? What's wrong? We weren't scheduled to talk until tonight."

"The Queen was on Port Broacia, not Genarg. The planet is ruined. Is everything in place?"

Crow nodded, swallowing hard as he saw the video himself. "We finished this morning. We have people inside to evacuate the workers when the time comes."

"The time's now. They can't keep getting away with this," Rainer said.

"Yes." Draif nodded. "Start moving, Crow."

"With pleasure." Crow disconnected.

———

Planet Vavis, Sugarworm System

Aiden Crow whistled as he walked out of the largest factory on Vavis, Cortez's small industrial planet. A blaring fire alarm echoed across the crowded shuttle lot in front of the building.

"Get behind the line," a security guard yelled. "We don't want a fucking lawsuit if this shit isn't just a glitch in the system."

"This is so annoying," the man beside him said. "It's going to take forever to catch up production after this."

"You know Mr. Arkwright will make us work overtime," a woman said.

Another worker snorted. "I've been working for twenty hours straight. Let me enjoy the damn break."

"A break that could cost us our jobs," the first man said. "They've made it pretty clear we either keep up production or get out."

Crow watched the time on his comm. One hand stayed in his pocket, finger ready to hit the detonation button. Two minutes passed quickly with the workers grumbling around him.

Crow's father had always told him an employer had to see their employee as a whole person, not just a cog in a wheel. Satisfied employees meant satisfied customers.

"I don't care if they fire me," the woman said. "It's not like this place pays well. I hear a person can take their family to Tammol for free and be set up with work and housing right away."

"Tammol? How do you contact them?"

Time to go, he thought and pushed down on the button.

The ground shook as the massive building shuddered, then started to crumble from the bottom up. It took only minutes for the factory to collapse, covered in flames.

Crow looked around. Not a lot of debris had made it to the crowd of workers, but a few had gotten hit. He noted their friends helping them stand and checking them over. They'd live. Some wouldn't, but each of the rebels had promised to make an effort to spare as many as they could.

The flames grew higher, and Crow could feel the heat from where he stood. *I'm sorry, Dad. I'm sorry I wasn't the son you wanted me to be. I'm sorry I didn't follow in your footsteps. I'm sorry I didn't protect you. I swear they'll pay for everything they've done.*

"Fuck," the security guard said, face pale. His comm chimed insistently.

Crow could hear the explosions coming from the other nearby factories and had to fight his smile. *Humans First will pay.*

He turned and started slowly making his way through the crowd, eyes on his comm as each of the teams checked in.

The two other people in his group met him at the shuttle, and they headed back to the ship.

Crow looked out the window. As far as he could see, Cortez's factories were burning and crumbling to the ground.

———

Charybdis Station, Anchors Rest System

THE COUNCIL GATHERED AROUND THE CONFERENCE table, watching the vid-screen projected in the middle.

A smiling woman stared at them, a still-smoking factory behind her.

"Only one day after Humans First led an attack against Port Broacia, Charybdis Station retaliated by destroying every last factory on Planet Vavis. Businessman Nelson Cortez owns the planet and used these factories to produce the goods of several companies owned by fellow humans. At the same time that Cortez's factories were destroyed, all of the factories owned by Sofus Hald on planets Rueal and Guthea were also demolished.

"Neither Hald nor Cortez could be reached for comment. These two men have recently come forward as members of Humans First. I think it is safe to say, Charybdis Station is stepping up to take on the large coalition that has callously murdered billions. All I can say is, thank you."

The report ended, and everyone exchanged looks. Draif knew this wasn't good. They hadn't been ready to go public.

"They're coming," Fasi said, face solemn. "Ninetta is shadowing the fleet carrying the Queen, and it looks like they're coming toward the Anchors Rest System."

"The galaxy thinks we're heroes," Councilman Mitchell said, shaking his head. "That's not a bad feeling, but damn, this isn't what we planned."

"How did they find out we were involved?" Councilwoman Jalina asked.

"One of the rebels was caught before he could leave." Draif glared at the table. "He didn't realize it wasn't Cortez's people that had him. An undercover journalist was there investigating the mistreatment of the factory workers, and she managed to trick him."

Lucas sat beside him, hand in his.

"Captain Ando," Councilwoman Rundell said, voice hard. "Look at me."

He looked up, meeting her gaze.

"The journalist doesn't realize she's just painted a target on our station, but this is a setback, not a disaster."

"How can you say that?" Draif's eyes widened.

"Right now, we're the people standing up to Humans First. We won't be alone for long." Councilwoman Rundell smiled. "You'll see."

Draif shook his head. "The Queen is something we can't fight. Any preparations I've made are useless if she's with them."

"She won't be with them," Finn said, looking up from his comm. "Hack and the others have a plan. They said to watch the news tonight."

———

A few days later, Draif and Lucas cuddled on the couch, watching Hack's video for a third time. Marmalade sat on Draif's lap, and Honey balanced on her haunches atop Lucas's head while Chutney watched from the back of the couch.

Hack's smiling face was projected from the tablet. *"Honestly, we thought the Queen was more dangerous than HF, but we were clearly wrong."*

Cordelia's beautiful face wore confusion well. *"What do you mean? Wasn't it difficult to take Genarg?"*

Hack grinned and shrugged. *"Not at all. The Queen wasn't here, and her Element Earth retreated into the planet to hide. Plus, we have the Element Death on our side. At this point, the Queen is superfluous. HF pulls her strings, and she basically belongs to them. Now, she has no real power of her own."*

Cordelia eyes widened almost comically. *"Goodness. What will you do with Genarg now that it belongs to you?"*

Hack grinned again. *"I was thinking of settling down and making it my own. There's a lot of resources to drill out of this planet. I think I can make a credit or two before it's a barren rock again. It even comes with a comfy throne."*

"Yeah," Lucas drawled. "That will get her attention."

An alert chimed on Draif's tablet, so he closed out Hack's video. "Looks like Ninetta sent an update."

Lucas leaned in and bit the tip of his ear. "What does she say?"

"Oh. Wow." Draif blinked, unsure if he was reading the message correctly.

"What?"

"The video worked. The Queen destroyed two thirds of the fleet and basically told HF to fuck off. She's going to Genarg with the remaining ships."

Draif was relieved but also scared to death. The Queen was headed for Leti.

Lucas took his tablet and set it aside. "I know that look, Draif. Hack and Leti will take care of the Queen, then come home. You have to believe that."

"I do." Draif cleared his throat and spoke again, stronger this time. "I do. They'll be home soon."

"They will." Lucas kissed the top of his head. "I have an idea."

"Yeah?"

"Our work against HF is public now, but there are benefits to that. One of the problems Ava keeps mentioning is a loss of morale across the galaxy. People see HF as this unstoppable force."

Draif considered Lucas's words. "That is a problem. We want them to join the fight."

"That journalist on Vextonar, I can't remember her name, but what if she went to Genarg and covered the confrontation with the Queen?"

"If we win, it will definitely give other planets and species the push they need to join in against HF," Draif said. "However, if we lose, then it would make the situation worse."

"If we lose," Lucas said slowly, "then it's all over. The Queen will keep killing for Humans First until there are no people left in the galaxy."

Draif buried his face against Lucas's chest. "Good point."

His comm chimed again, and he took the call. Chad Ige's face was projected from Draif's wrist communicator.

"Ige, Lucas is with me," Draif said, giving the man warning. Lucas knew about all Draif's contacts, but it had become habit to keep secrets.

Ige grinned. "That's fine with me. You need to celebrate with your mate, Draif. Humans First are a fucking tangled mess. Cortez and Hald are destitute, and Malone's finances aren't looking so great thanks to Gus. Goel is struggling to keep things together, but more ships are leaving the fleet here in Rueal every day, and the Queen just destroyed more than half of the fleet heading away from Port Broacia."

"We just saw a video of it," Draif said, smiling.

Ige looked like he wanted to dance. "It was beautiful. I was in the room with Malone. She ordered the Queen to ignore General Hackett's video and continue to your station. The Queen just looked at her and said *I'm done with you*. Then ships exploded, and Malone collapsed back in her chair. She was shocked, Draif. Malone and the others actually thought they controlled the Queen."

Draif exchanged a look with Lucas. "We wondered how that was working. Hack and the others figured out the Queen wanted Humans First to think they were in charge. She's been manipulating them from the start. Her goal was simply to cause as much chaos and bloodshed in the galaxy as possible."

"That explains why they've made such stupid business decisions," Ige said, rubbing his chin. "Now, HF is crumbling in on itself. The only things holding it up are the big four and the support from Rueal and Vextonar."

"Crow and some friends of his are heading to Rueal now," Draif said. "They're going to work on sabotaging Malone's businesses there."

"I'll help him as much as I can. Poor Teresa Malone has been having a lot of mysterious financial trouble lately. It's been beautiful." Ige's expression turned serious. "Charybdis Station is on the big four's radar, Draif. More importantly, so are you. They know your name, and they know you've been responsible for their troubles."

"How?" Lucas asked. "How do they know about Draif?"

"That mole of yours heard more than we thought he did. He didn't know enough to share *how* you were doing it, but he knew you and a woman named Ava have been working against Humans First."

The air beside the couch shimmered, and Bendix appeared. He bent and waved to Ige. "Hey, man. We have a guard on Draif all the time. We'll keep him safe. I'll get someone on Ava now."

Ige's eyes grew big. "Where did you come from?"

Draif snorted. "Charybdis Station has some impressive shielding technology. Bendix here is supposed to tell us when he's on guard duty though."

Bendix sat on the couch and stretched an arm across the back. "Where's the fun in that?"

Ige laughed. "He has a point, Draif. Oh, I've been meaning to ask, why does your mate have a Fire Veil Dragon on his head?"

18

TWO MONTHS LATER

"Be careful, Morgan." Lucas tried to keep the worry out of his voice. His friend knew the danger he was going into, and he didn't need Lucas's worry on top of his own.

"We will." Morgan ran a hand through his blond hair. "Wyatt and the other doctors and medics will be stationed away from the fighting. The rest of us will be in the middle of it. I won't lie. I'm scared. We have a plan, but ultimately, either we win, or we die."

"You'll win," Lucas said, voice full of certainty. "You have a plan, allies, and a hell of a lot to lose."

Lucas didn't understand how he could be so worried and so proud all at once. Humans First and the Queen had done so much damage to the galaxy, but Charybdis Station was finally able to stand up to them. His mind kept going back to Brinanda. The woman had sold out Charybdis Station for credits, but she truly thought they would all fail.

"Have there been any other attacks on Ava, Draif, and the Lord Admiral?"

Lucas snarled. "Three attempts on Fasi, two on Ava, and five on Draif. Between Half Moon and the Blue Fleet, we have them covered in guards, and we've been able to stop each attempt."

"I'll be glad when this is finally over."

"Me too. Draif already agreed to take a week off and go to Cardinal's Hold with me when this is over." Lucas shook his head. "I wish I could be there with you. I don't like watching from a distance."

Morgan grinned. "You just want to show off for your mate."

Lucas sniffed. "I don't know what you're talking about."

Morgan just laughed at him.

Wyatt's face appeared over Morgan's shoulder. "Will you stay with Estella and the twins during the battle, Lucas? The twins are too young to know what's happening, but Estella needs all the support she can get."

"I will. We're gathering everyone together at Hack and Leti's house. I'll sit with your girls. Keep me updated on your status."

Morgan nodded, then the vid-screen went blank.

Lucas took a breath and let it out slowly. Sitting out of this fight was shit.

He checked on Honey. The small dragon slept with Marmalade in the middle of Lucas and Draif's bed. Chutney watched over them from the window seat.

He found Draif in his office talking with Leti. The

Druffle were quiet today, as if they knew the station was holding its breath.

"I love you, Leti. You *will* come back. You have your lucky baby bunnies and Princess Buttercup," Draif said.

Leti's freckled face filled Draif's vid-screen. "We'll make it, Draif. I still need to bring Elril home to meet his brothers and sisters."

"Rizzie isn't happy with you, by the way," Draif said. "She would much rather have another sister."

"She'll love him when she meets him."

"I didn't say she didn't love him." Draif smiled softly. "Riz already has plans to throw him a welcome party and share some of her stuffies with him. She just would rather Elril was another girl."

Leti giggled happily. "I love my kids. Now, read me your newest poem. I need some happy before going out there."

Draif cleared his throat. "Abdominal V / Leads to happiness and fun / Lucas's dick. Yum."

Leti's eyes watered. "A haiku? Draif, that was so beautiful."

Hack's voice came through the line. "Leti, it's time."

Leti gave Draif one more smile. "I love you, Draify. I know my kids are safe with you, even if the worst happens. We'll update you all as soon as we can."

The screen went blank, and Lucas cleared his throat.

Draif looked up, tears filling his eyes. "I can't lose Leti, Lucas. I just can't."

Lucas went and pulled his mate into his arms. "You won't. Now, we have some kids to reassure. I also think we should talk about your poetry. It's... amazing."

Together, they went to Leti's house. The large living room and kitchen were full of people. The Council and their families were interspersed with people from the Yellow and Blue Fleets.

Councilman Delino sat beside Becca, one of the three creators of the Bracken. The woman had created the Bracken named Meggie and considered the android her daughter. Lucas absently noted the two held hands. It looked like the rumor about them being a couple was more than a rumor.

Gregor, the third creator of the Bracken, sat on Becca's other side. The man looked a mess, and Lucas knew he was worried about his Bracken daughter, Sax.

"Uncle Draify!" Sami ran through the room of people and jumped into Draif's arms.

"Hey, buddy." Draif hugged him tightly.

Lucas steered them toward a seat. "Let's sit with Estella and the others."

Morgan and Wyatt's adopted daughter sat with Mo and the other kids. She was nestled against Mo's side, and the boy had his arm around her shoulders. The two were a few years apart in age, but somehow, they had managed to become best friends. *How old do you have to be to recognize a life mate*, he thought.

Leander and his family squeezed into a spot near them.

Chay sat next to Draif and hugged him. "Your friends will be okay, Draif."

Draif gave Lucas a panicked look.

Lucas mimed hugging, and Draif finally returned his brother's hug. "Thanks, Chay."

Leander and his family were settling into the station well. Leander had quickly found work in the Blue Sector's gardens. It wasn't like anything the man had ever done in the past, but he completely loved it.

Sybil and Tempest were working in Juniper's Diner, and Shae had confided that the two women were lifesavers. Tempest served customers while Sybil took over the kitchen.

Innis scooted in close to Rose. The two had become good friends. Both he and Chay had a lot of catching up to do with their education, but the boys were smart and didn't mind work.

Leander sat next to Lucas and took his hand. "I know you're worried too, Lucas. I'm here if you need to talk."

Sybil reached over and hugged first him, then Draif. "Trust in your friends, boys. From all I've heard, they're amazing and determined people."

Lucas fought a smile. Leander and Sybil were determined to become his parents as well as Draif's.

Hours passed as they sat and talked together. Shae, Sybil, and Ma made sure they were all fed. Eventually, the crowd moved to the backyard so the kids could run around and play with Wobble and Trixie.

Then the call came. Fasi and Draif's comms chimed at the same time.

Draif fumbled, hands trembling as he read the message. "The Queen is dead."

Lucas grinned as the house practically shook with the cheering.

Fasi stood and raised his hands. "We won, but we lost people."

He started reading out names. Lucas recognized each one from Charybdis Station.

"Hazel?" Estella's eyes watered. "She's gone?" Lucas went to her and held her as she cried.

Bendix bent his head as Fasi named the Half Moon assassins that had fallen, including Clara, and he yelped when Pops and Ma both hugged him between them.

"We're sorry, Bendix. I know Beol and you cherish each of your people," Ma said.

Fasi finished listing the dead. "Most of our people are wounded and will need to recover before they can come home."

"Morrick? Is he… Is he alive?" Val asked.

Fasi nodded. "He survived, Val."

"Jen Rally is releasing videos," Draif said. He hurried to the vid-screen in the living room and pulled up the first one.

They piled into the house and watched the journalist interview people about their interactions with the Queen and Humans First. Several humans told of loved ones stolen and sold on Vextonar.

Clara told some stories of growing up on Union Station and how she felt about its destruction. Ma and Pops held Bendix as he watched the interview, eyes full of sadness. The other Half Moon assassins stayed close to him.

Hack and Leti told about the discovery of the artifact and their journey in figuring out what it was.

Remy told about his resurrection and his experiences with Charybdis Station.

Death stood with his son Wyatt and told about his history with the Queen.

Fire and Sebastian talked about Crellic Shamanism.

Earth… Earth told about his love of a woman long gone. A woman that would be horrified by the Queen's actions.

A short time later, another video came through. They watched Remy's rite of passage.

Lucas wasn't sure what to think about shamanism, but he had to admit the rite of passage looked interesting. This one was a lot different from Sebastian's. It was a party rather than a show of proof of shamanism.

The video then moved on to more interviews as everyone prepared for the Queen's arrival.

"That's Meggie and Dad," Nessa said, bouncing. "They're life mates."

Meggie and Dannol told the journalist about the Bracken and about discovering they were life mates. Lucas couldn't help but smile at the joy in Meggie's eyes when she talked about having a new daughter.

On the screen, Meggie smiled nervously. *"I wasn't sure I could have a life mate. You have to have a soul, and us Bracken aren't like everyone else. We feel and think for ourselves, but I didn't know if we had souls. I wanted to think we did, but how do you prove something like that?"* She looked at Dannol. *"I knew I loved my mom and my friends. When I met Dannol, I didn't know what was going on at first. He became my heartbeat, and I realized I had to have a soul to feel something so beautiful."*

Becca started crying. "That's my daughter. Gods, look at how happy she is."

Nessa sniffled and hugged Becca. "I can't wait until she gets home."

A little while later, they sent the children to bed. The video of the battle was all over the news stations.

"Look at Olla fly," Draif said proudly as they watched the Blue Moyra soar through the sky, shields gone. Olla dodged missiles and flew circles around the enemy ships, firing shot after shot of her own.

"That's our girl," Anders yelled, cheering with the rest of the crew. Even Ginger looked impressed, and Lucas knew she dreaded Olla returning. She was happy on Draif's crew.

The land battle was much more chaotic.

Lucas blinked. "Fuck me, that's Leti on Princess Buttercup's back." Maia sat behind him, pulse cannon firing at the enemy ships still in the air.

"That's Leti?" Leander asked, eyes wide. "Goodness, I expected him to be gentle and sweet."

"He is," Draif said, laughing. "Princess is the one that's a badass."

The video focused on the battle with the Queen, and Lucas's eyes caught on Sebastian. The man was only a couple of months away from giving birth, but he stood there, Fire's Elemental form circling him, while he held the Queen's firewall back, face full of pure determination.

Alois stood at his side, guarding him as HF soldiers and other creatures attacked.

"Sebastian is officially my hero," Finn said, eyes wide. "Oh, damn, look at Meggie."

The Bracken used a pair of Beck's altered gravitational boots to jump in and out of the battle with the wounded. They watched her pick up a wounded Dru and jump away.

The other two Bracken, Icarus and Sax, fought in tandem together, taking out an impressive number of enemies.

"Look at my little girl," Gregor said, sniffling. "Sax is the best Charybdis soldier in the galaxy."

Lucas stiffened when Remy raised his hands, and the dead HF soldiers stood back up. He jumped. "Fucking zombies! I knew there were going to be fucking zombies."

"Calm down, babe." Draif leaned over and kissed his cheek. "The zombies are on our side."

"That's how it starts," Lucas muttered, sulking.

The battle was tense and reached a stalemate. Lucas's friends could hold the Queen back, but they couldn't move forward.

Then Meggie jumped to Beck. Lucas expected her to pick Beck up, but she stopped and looked through the flames at the Queen and poor Earth.

"What is she doing?" Becca asked.

Lucas saw the resolve in Meggie's eyes as she braced herself and jumped into the Queen's fire.

"Meggie, no!" Becca covered her mouth. "Oh gods."

"She's not dead, Becca. I promise," Fasi said, voice full of emotion. "Your daughter saved us all."

They watched her kill the Queen and fall to the ground, burning.

Fasi moved to rest a hand on Becca's shoulder. "Leti said she is severely injured, but she'll live. Beck will do his best to fix her"

"Skin," Becca said, swallowing. "She'll need skin and hair. Oh, my sweet girl."

Gregor held back a sob. "I'll start working on her nerves and muscle tissue."

Delino wrapped his arms around Becca. "She's alive. That's what's important."

Lucas watched Death kneel at Meggie's side and hold her molten hot hand. He stood, then leaned over to whisper in Draif's ear. "I'll be right back."

Draif's eyes were stuck on the video as the journalist surveyed the battleground. "Okay. I'll be here."

Lucas left the house and rode the tram to the Enforcement Center. His mind kept replaying Meggie's jump into the fire. She had been afraid. She hadn't *wanted* to die. Meggie had just found her mate and had a new daughter to meet.

The halls were quiet. Groups of enforcers gathered together, watching the battle on their comms and tablets.

Lucas made it to the cell blocks easily, the guards nodding as he passed them. Soon enough, he stood in front of the cell of Brinanda, the former Councilwoman.

She looked up, curiosity filling her eyes. "What are you doing here, lieutenant?"

Lucas didn't say anything. He pulled the video up on his comm and let her watch it.

Brinanda grew pale, and she sat hard on the cot in her cell. "They did it. The Queen is dead."

"Look at her, Brinanda," Lucas said, replaying Meggie's jump. "Look at the person you called a soulless husk. Look at the woman that saved the fucking galaxy. The person you would have sold to the enemy to be taken apart and studied like a lab rat."

Brinanda shook, but she didn't answer.

"When I watched this, when I saw what Meggie did, all I could think about was that *you*, a woman I once respected, thought Meggie was either a few parts bolted together or some kind of abomination."

"She killed the Queen?"

"Yes," he hissed. "I know they'll just exile you, but I want you to know that you lost more than your position on Charybdis Station. Because you had no integrity, you lost the chance to be on the winning side in this war. Good luck finding a planet to take you in after this."

Lucas turned on his heels and left, shaking with his anger. He didn't know why he was so mad at Brinanda. There were too many other things to focus on.

He was so proud of Meggie, so proud of Charybdis Station.

By the time he got home, Fasi and the Council were getting drunk. He didn't see Draif, so he went to their house and found him in his office.

Ige was on his office vid-screen. "I was with Malone again today. They saw the videos of the battle. They're furious and afraid, Draif. Goel is sending every ship stationed in Vextonar to Rueal. From here, Cortez's son Beldon will gather all of HF's fleets and fly straight to Charybdis Station. They know there's no recovering from this. They just want your station destroyed."

Lucas met Draif's eyes from the door.

His mate's smile was predatory. "Let them come. It's time to end this."

19

ONE AND A HALF MONTHS LATER

Draif pressed a trail of kisses along Lucas's hip. His mate was spread across the bed, naked and waiting for Draif's mouth.

He smoothed a hand over Lucas's robotic leg and his mate shivered. Draif could look at Lucas all day long. The man's long limbs and smooth skin made his mouth water.

He dipped his head and licked Lucas's inner thigh and wrapped his fingers around his hard dick, pumping him.

Lucas's breathing stuttered. "Fuck, love."

Draif licked the tip of Lucas's dick, then cupped his balls in his other hand, squeezing lightly. There was nothing better than his mate's taste and smell. Absolutely nothing.

He licked and sucked Lucas's dick for several minutes, loving the sounds his mate made. He pressed his own hips down against the bed, close to coming.

Lucas's hands gripped the headboard when Draif swallowed his dick again, and Draif could hear Lucas's claws digging into the wood.

Lucas groaned as he shot down Draif's throat. Draif's own hips twitched when he came against the sheets. Watching his mate come was the hottest thing Draif had ever seen.

Lucas let go of the headboard and pulled Draif up his body for a kiss. "Love you."

"Love you too," Draif whispered.

The past month had been hectic to say the least. Draif knew he had to help Ava, Fasi, and the Council make plans, but damn if he didn't just want to spend time with Lucas. Their home was finally *a home*. Their kids might be two cats and a dragon, but they were still Draif's family.

His siblings came to visit all the time, and Sami and Rizzie probably spent more time at Draif and Lucas's house than their own. Draif loved it.

All he needed was Leti home. Unfortunately, they were still a couple of weeks away.

Draif rubbed his face against Lucas's chest. Humans First, on the other hand, would reach Charybdis any day now.

His comm buzzed, and Lucas grabbed it before he could. "Hey, Chad."

Ige snorted. "Did I interrupt something?"

Lucas growled. "Yes, you did, but my mate likes you, so I'll try to forgive you."

Ige laughed. "Thanks."

Draif slapped Lucas's shoulder, then kissed the slight mark he had made. "Any updates?"

Ige's eyes drifted down for a moment before he met Draif's gaze. "You know I've become *friends* with Beldon Cortez, right?"

Draif wrinkled his nose. "I'm truly sorry you had to do that."

"Me too." Ige rubbed his forehead. "He's a cruel, arrogant bastard. We've talked quite a bit."

"Has his battle plans changed any?"

Ige rolled his eyes. "No. Beldon is lazy as hell and is just relying on the flagship's captain to make the decisions."

"Otto said you all would arrive sometime tomorrow," Lucas said, scratching an ear. "This will be over soon, thank the gods."

Ige smiled. "I'm looking forward to seeing Charybdis Station."

"We'll take you to Juniper's Diner," Draif said. "You can meet my sister and my stepmom."

Ige nodded. "I'll take you up on that." He looked uncomfortable for a moment. "During one of our talks, Beldon mentioned something from his past. He told me about a bed-slave in training he seduced. He couldn't remember his name, but he described the boy, and it was a boy. He was only fifteen."

Draif flushed. Beldon had been with many boys just like him.

"Beldon remembered this boy in particular because the boy fell in love with him."

Lucas reached for his hand and squeezed it.

"What's your point?" Draif asked.

"Beldon told me a lot of things about this boy and how he was treated. He told me how the boy killed two trainers and how the others held him down. How they brutalized him before maiming him. The bastard thought it was hilarious."

"Of course he did," Lucas said, eyes full of pain.

Draif leaned up and kissed his mate's cheek. He didn't like that Lucas hurt for him. Draif couldn't change his past. All he could do was move forward, and dwelling on that time wasn't good for anyone.

Ige nodded. "You know about Evelyn."

"Yeah," Draif said. "Goel and Hald will both die. I can promise you that."

"So will Beldon Cortez," Ige said, eyes full of ice. "I swear it. During the battle tomorrow, you'll have to focus on all the moving pieces. Me? My ship will focus on one thing. The captains of my fleet know what to do. They don't need my direction."

"Ige." Draif hated that his voice sounded so feeble. "It's not important."

"No," Lucas said. "It is important. Ige, if you're able to take that son of a bitch out, I'll be in your debt."

"No debts," Ige said, voice harsh. "Evelyn would have liked you, Draif. She would have admired your wit and bravery."

A quiet chime sounded in the room – the doorbell.

"Sounds like you have company," Ige said. "I'll let you know if any of Beldon's plans change."

"Thank you, Ige," Draif said, swallowing back tears. He hated fucking crying.

The call ended, and the chime sounded again.

Lucas groaned. "We haven't even had breakfast yet."

Draif poked Lucas's ribs. "Time to get up. Go make me coffee. I'll chase off whoever's at the door."

By the time Draif had thrown on clothes and brushed his teeth, the doorbell had chimed two more times. *Impatient fuckers*, he thought.

He opened the door, then froze. Fasi and all six Council members stood on his small porch. "Um, I thought we were meeting in our conference room?"

Fasi smiled, eyes twinkling. "May we come in, Draif?"

Draif shook his head and held the door open. "Yeah. Of course. Come in."

Councilwoman Rundell looked around. "It's a lot quieter than last time."

Lucas yelled from the kitchen. "Damn it, Trixie. Come back here."

Leti's goat bleated as she ran from the kitchen and headed to the staircase. Honey was perched on the bottom stair post and leaned back to let out a deep belch of fire. Trixie ran straight up the stairs, unconcerned with the small dragon.

Councilwoman Rundell laughed. "Maybe I spoke too soon."

Draif covered his face with his hands. "I'd like to say this is just bad timing, but Trixie really likes going upstairs, and Honey's a brat."

Lucas came out of the kitchen and paused when he saw their guests. "Oh, uh, hey. I didn't know we were meeting here today. Can I get you all anything?"

"Some pants would be nice," Councilman Mitchell said, chuckling. "For yourself, of course."

Lucas looked down. He wore a pair of tight-fitting briefs. "Good idea."

He ran up the steps, and Honey let out another belch of fire.

"Chutney," Draif yelled. "Come control your daughter!"

The large tomcat slowly made his way down the staircase. He stopped and gave Honey a hard look. The baby dragon climbed off the stair post and did her best to look contrite.

Draif sighed. "Have a seat. What can I do for you all?"

The Council and Fasi sat, and Councilman Delino leaned forward, bracing his arms on his legs. "It's come to our attention that we neglected to think of all of Charybdis Station's needs as we structured our government."

"What do you mean?"

"We've made the decision to bring Half Moon into our ranks," Councilwoman Jalina said. "They will be the Full Moon division and will focus on covert operations. Fasi told General Hackett and, well, General Beol about it a few days ago. Is it General Beol? I don't know the man's last name."

"It'll be Brackenridge as soon as he gets back to the station," Fasi said with a shrug.

Draif grinned. "That's great. They're more than just assassins, and their skills and resources will be a good thing for Charybdis Station."

"It's timely too," Councilman Delino said. "Bendix has his people in place. We'll give the order when the younger Cortez and his fleet get here. We don't want him running when HF's leadership dies."

Draif couldn't wait for this to be over. He wanted that damn vacation with Lucas.

"We've also created positions of leadership for our agriculture, medical, diplomatic, and economic divisions," Councilman Warren said. "Our government is in its infancy, and we're expanding and adapting to what our people need."

"I'm glad to hear that."

"One position that we haven't filled yet is my second-in-command," Fasi said. "With the recent assassination attempts, we've realized it would be wise to have multiple back up plans or, well, a potential successor in place."

Draif frowned. "Has there been another attack?"

Councilman Warren shook his head. "No. We don't expect to lose Fasi anytime soon, but this whole situation has made us more aware that it's always possible. Plus, we're expanding so quickly, and Fasi is just one person. The Lord Admiral could use some help."

"Okay." Draif could see the benefit of Fasi having a second-in-command equal in position to the four generals – someone who could help him with the day-to-day duties of running the station. "Do you want me to start researching and doing some background checks? Charybdis Station is full of good candidates."

Fasi smiled softly. "There are several people I would be proud to have at my side, Draif, but we actually have someone in mind."

Councilwoman Rundell reached over and poked him in the arm. "We want you."

Draif gave her a puzzled look. Surely, she didn't mean they wanted him to be Fasi's second-in-command. "You want me for what?"

Fasi grinned. "We want you to be Vice Admiral of Charybdis Station."

Draif blinked. "Huh?"

Councilwoman Rundell sighed. "I really thought he was smarter than this."

Councilwoman Holli rolled her eyes and elbowed the elderly Siren. "He's in shock, Rundell. Can you blame him?"

"You want *me* to be your second-in-command?"

"Yes," Fasi said, nodding. "I was voted in by the Council, and they've voted you in as well. When I retire—"

"Many years from now," Councilman Delino interrupted.

Fasi snorted. "When I retire many years from now, the Council will vote in a new Lord Admiral and Vice Admiral."

"Who knows," Councilman Mitchell said, voice sly, "you may be voted in as Lord Admiral one day."

Draif leaned back in his seat, completely

unsurprised when Marmalade meowed and hopped into his lap. His cat always seemed to know when he needed her.

"Are you sure? I'm just… I'm just me. There are so many people who have been here longer. People who would be excellent for the position."

"We have a number of excellent candidates," Councilwoman Rundell said and smiled at Draif. "… including you."

Councilwoman Holli tsked. "Really, Captain Ando. Not only have you done so much to fight against Humans First, our enemy, but you've also worked with Half Moon, engineering, and your young friend Gus to increase and improve the station's security. Our financial advisers tell us you even send them investment ideas and all types of information to help keep Charybdis Station solvent."

"You have a damn good head on your shoulders, son," Fasi said proudly.

"I was a bed-slave," Draif said, almost whispering. "I was born into slavery."

Councilwoman Jalina stood and stomped her foot. "Why should that matter? Charybdis Station's never cared one bit about a species or personal backgrounds. It's always been about a person's grit and integrity."

Fasi gave him a pointed look. "You, Draif Ando, are full of grit and integrity."

"You know you want to accept, love," Lucas said from the bottom of the stairs, fully dressed this time. "My mate, the Vice Admiral of Charybdis Station. Holy catnip, Draif. Imagine all the things you could get up to in that position."

"Are you sure?" Draif looked at each person in the room. "We haven't defeated HF yet."

"We will," Councilman Delino said, voice sure. "Tomorrow, our fleets will meet Beldon Cortez in battle, and we will decimate the last remnants of those murderous bastards. Of that I have no doubt."

"I would like my Vice Admiral at my side during the battle," Fasi said. "What do you say?"

Draif slowly smiled. "As long as we take my ship."

Fasi whooped and stood, pulling Draif up and into a hug.

Councilman Warren pulled his tablet out. "I'll let Pops know to prepare the Blue Raven to be our flagship. It'll need extra security and weapons."

Draif met Lucas's eyes over Fasi's shoulder. His mate looked extraordinarily proud of him.

"It'll need a new name," Lucas said. "The Blue Raven is part of the Blue Fleet. The Vice Admiral's ship should be called the Black Heron."

———

Later that day, Draif watched Lucas and Chay chase after Sami and his friend Almond in the backyard. The light glinted off his mate's fangs as Lucas growled deeply, claws raised in the air.

Sami and Almond giggled and ran toward Wobble, though Draif didn't know what the llama could do to save them.

Leti watched from Draif's tablet.

"I can't believe Sami has a friend already. I can't believe he's in school and has already grown another two inches." Leti's lip trembled. "I miss my babies."

"You'll be home in a couple of weeks." Draif rubbed his chest, missing his friend. "How is Sebastian doing?" Draif and Leti's friend had just given birth.

Leti perked up. "He's fine. Alois and he finally agreed on a name – Mordecai. I'm calling him Mordy, and I don't care if they hate it. He's so cute, Draif. It almost makes me want another baby. Almost."

"Beol doing okay?"

"Yeah. He hasn't admitted I'm his best friend yet, but he will."

"I meant is he doing okay since he's pregnant with twins and due soon?"

Leti laughed. "He's as grumpy as ever and can't wait for the babies to come. The only people he doesn't constantly snap at are Beck and the kids. Any time he gets too grumpy, we just hand him Aketil. That little Crell has her daddies wrapped around her finger."

"I'm glad to hear it." Draif bit his lip. "Now that you're closer to home, there are a few things I need to tell you, so you're prepared."

Leti's eyes narrowed. "I know you got Pepper a pet. No one will tell us what it is, but Will isn't happy. I, on the other hand, am just fine with it. Every baby needs a pet."

"That's one of the things," Draif said, nodding. "While we were on Derelict, Lucas found two baby Fire Veil Dragons."

Leti gasped. "Those poor things! Did he get them? Tell me he got them."

"He did." Draif made a face. "Honey is one of them. She came with a cat nanny."

Leti raised his fist in the air. "Yes! Another baby for Princess Buttercup to raise. Wait. What exactly is a cat nanny?"

Leti's Fyrling, Jenks, ran into his hand and sputtered for a second before continuing her slow buzz around Leti's head.

"Sorry, Jenks!" Leti covered his mouth, eyes wide. "My Fyrling reminds me of Finn and Lucas on their catnip days."

Draif snickered. "She really does, and a cat nanny is a large tomcat that mothers a baby dragon."

Leti chuckled. "Is that Chutney?"

"Yes. I'll send you some pictures of them. They're all napping with Marmalade right now, or maybe they're burning the house down. I'm not sure."

"Send them right now," Leti ordered.

Draif sighed but did as he was told.

"Okay, back on topic." Leti shook his finger. "Tell me your other secrets."

"Well, Pepper's pet is the second Fire Veil Dragon."

Leti squealed. "That's perfect. Oh sugar cookies, Will is going to be so mad."

"She loves Aagy." Draif turned the tablet to the corner of the yard.

Pepper played in a sandbox with Milo and the other younger neighborhood children. Aagy lay in the middle of the babies, letting them cover him in sand. Moses and Shae watched from a bench nearby.

"Princess, look," Leti said and moved his tablet so Princess could see. "There's your little brother, Aagy. Isn't he cute?"

Princess blinked, then hissed.

Leti laughed. "Don't worry, baby boy. You're still my sweetheart."

Draif rolled his eyes. "Come on, Princess. He really needs your help. He doesn't know how to change sizes, and he's an orphan. You need to step up here, buddy. He didn't come with a cat nanny."

Princess huffed and laid his head on Leti's shoulder.

"He'll be a good big brother," Leti said, petting his head.

Draif cleared his throat. "In other news, I can't remember if I told you that my dad and his family are now living in Lucas's house."

Leti grinned. "You did, and I'm so glad you get along with him."

Draif shifted his tablet again, and Leti laughed when he saw Leander bent over one of the flowerbeds, doing his best to repair some damage Trixie had caused. The goat leaned over his shoulder, watching as he worked.

"Yeah. I really can't wait to meet him."

Draif turned the tablet back around. "Did you know that Sybil and Tempest are helping Shae run Juniper's Diner? They love it."

"Juniper told me he was looking forward to having

the help when he gets back." Leti smiled fondly. "I want to be home."

Draif rested his chin on his fist. "I also decided to take a different position at the station."

"No! Will loves that you're one of his captains. He brags on you all the time. Is it those three turd heads that were bothering you? Did they pressure you into resigning?"

"Reed, Yeardley, and Wyther aren't so bad," Draif said, shrugging. "The position I took is working with Fasi."

Leti watched him closely, excitement filling his eyes. "Draify, what's the position?"

"Vice Admiral of Charybdis Station."

Draif winced when Leti yelled loud enough to startle Mo's rabbit, Abbot, from his nap next to Draif's chair. "Sorry, Abbot."

The rabbit gave him a confused look, then hopped over to sit with Mo and Pops. The two were talking about installing Druffle tunnels in Selene, Morgan, and Dru's houses while they were gone.

"Draif, I can't believe it." Leti paused. "Actually, I really can believe it. You *are* the most amazing person in the galaxy."

"You may be a little biased."

Leti shook his head. "Nope. Just ask Lucas."

Draif watched his mate toss Almond in the air, then catch him. "He may be slightly biased too."

Leti laughed. "Just accept your greatness."

"Leti?"

Leti quieted down and watched him, letting Draif gather his thoughts.

"You remember when we met?"

"Technically, we first met when you were unconscious, but I remember when you woke up."

"I was in so much pain, but you were gentle when you tended my wounds. I remember thinking you were a servant at first."

Leti snorted. "I probably acted like one."

"When the doctor listed out my injuries, you cried for me."

"Draify," Leti said, eyes watering. "I was angry enough I would have killed those people myself if I'd been able to."

"I remember Princess Buttercup laying beside me while I healed. I remember you reading books and telling stories. No one had ever paid so much attention to me unless they wanted something in return. You didn't have to love me, but you did."

Leti smiled. "I'll always love you, Draif. You're my best friend and my brother."

"I love you, Leti. I think loving you saved me. I didn't want to live anymore when Beldon and the training compound were finished with me. Then, loving you and seeing you and Hack together gave me the courage to love Lucas. You've given me so much."

"You're making me cry." Leti tried to wipe the tears from his face, but they fell too fast.

"I just wanted you to know how much I appreciate you. *You* are the most amazing person in the galaxy, not me."

Leti sniffled. "Do you want me to read you my newest poem?"

"Yes, please."

Leti nodded and wiped at his eyes. "I wrote it this morning, and it's six stanzas long. Here's the first one. My pleasure is a hot coal / Will's penis moves my soul / His turgid member is impressive / or maybe I'm just obsessive."

Draif closed his eyes. "Beautiful."

20

A FEW HOURS FROM CHARYBDIS STATION

Draif stood with Lucas on the bridge of the Black Heron at the front of the Charybdis Fleet. Honey was perched on Lucas's shoulder, doing her best to look fierce, even though she carried a stuffed chew toy in her mouth. That morning, she had let them know, in no uncertain terms, that she was coming along.

A large fleet from Haven had stayed behind to defend the station, but with a little luck, that wouldn't be needed. Renee hadn't been pleased to stay behind, but the Council had insisted someone remain to lead them if the station was attacked.

The majority of the Blue Fleet and the Yellow Fleet appeared to be missing, but Draif knew they were just... busy. However, each planet in the system had sent ships to aid in the battle. They gathered behind the Black Heron.

Ginger had their leaders on call on one of the screens, awaiting orders.

Bendix lounged in one of the chairs, legs stretched out in front of him. His tablet was in his hands, and he looked bored. His Fyrling slept curled up on Bendix's stomach. Fasi sat in the lieutenant's chair. Despite Draif's protests, Fasi had refused to take the captain's chair.

"Here they come," Ginger said, voice hard. Her ears were laid back on her head, and she practically hissed.

The HF Fleet was large and had at least a third more ships than currently flew with Charybdis Station.

Draif knew there were two separate, smaller fleets holding back. Beldon's captain liked to have a back-up plan. Fortunately, so did Draif.

"The flagship is hailing us," Ginger said.

Fasi nodded. "Let's see what he has to say."

Beldon Cortez's smug face appeared on the large vid-screen at the front of the bridge.

"So," Beldon said, eyes full of disdain. "This is the rabble that protects Charybdis Station. Tell me, Lord Admiral, do you regret allowing two of your fleets to leave your station two months ago? It was a foolish decision."

Draif gasped, trembling, and clutched his tablet to his chest. "How did you know that?"

Lucas's claws settled on his lower back, and Draif's mate scratched gently. Draif figured it was his way of laughing at Draif's acting skills.

Beldon looked him over. "You look familiar." The man shrugged. "It's no matter. Humans will always outsmart you lesser beings. We may have suffered some setbacks, but we will come back stronger than before. You and your pitiful station are simply an annoying fly I'm here to swat."

Fasi cleared his throat. "I don't suppose you'll surrender?"

Beldon laughed. "Aren't you quaint?"

Fasi looked at Draif. "Was that a no? I don't really speak arrogant asshole."

"No," Beldon said, rolling his eyes. "We will not surrender to the likes of you."

Bendix sighed happily and tapped a message out on his tablet.

Draif sent a signal from his own tablet, and the shields dropped from the Yellow Fleet's ships. They encircled the large fleet. Audre's face appeared on the screen of leaders. "Lord Admiral, I believe this evens our odds."

"You really should have surrendered, Cortez," Fasi said, shaking his head. "Would you like to reconsider?"

Ships approached from behind Cortez's fleet, and Beldon smiled again, eyes sharp. "You don't think I was so foolish as to not prepare for this, do you? My colleagues approach, Lord Admiral. How about you surrender? Oh, never mind. I'd rather just destroy you."

Draif gave the man a sympathetic look. "I'm sorry to be the one to tell you this, but one of your colleagues had an accident."

Ginger pulled up a screen and connected it to Beldon's ship. Finn sprawled in the captain's chair of the flagship of one of the approaching fleets. "Hey Beldon, buddy. Captain Onion Breath didn't make it through the fight last night. He's piled up with the rest of your dead in the commons of this lovely ship. Lord Admiral, can I keep it? It's so shiny and new. Oh, and we have over a hundred more here."

The smaller fleet spread out, surrounding the lower side of the HF Fleet. The ships of the Blue Fleet, dropped their shields, becoming visible and filling in the gaps between Finn's stolen ships.

Beldon paled, shaking. "How did you... How did you find them?"

Draif smiled coldly. "Us lesser beings have a bit of intelligence."

Plus, Ige told us, Draif thought, doing his best not to dance around the bridge.

The second, smaller HF reinforcement fleet approached Cortez's right side, and the hope on Beldon's face almost made Draif feel sorry for him.

Ginger patched through the fleet's captain.

Ige grinned. "There's a lot of allies behind you, Draif. Your Lord Admiral sure knows how to make friends."

"Ige," Beldon said, voice harsh, "you *know* this garbage?"

Ige's face turned cold. "Draif Ando is twice the person you will ever be, Cortez. I've dreamed of this moment since supposedly joining your repulsive coalition."

Draif noticed the captain of Beldon's flagship reading his comm, face pale.

"You'll die for this, Ige," Beldon said, shaking with anger. "I'll kill you myself."

"Do you honestly think you're going to make it out of this, Cortez?" Ige asked.

Beldon sniffed. "Oh, I will. Before the day is out, either Goel or my father will put a contract on your head."

Bendix stood. "Funny you should say that, you overdeveloped cumshot. I think your captain needs to show you something."

———

Silverlight System, Planet Vextonar

DORIS WILLABY PARKED THE DELIVERY SHUTTLE AT THE back of the huge estate after security had thoroughly searched both her and the shuttle.

Enforcement officers patrolled the elegant landscape, a dark spot to the otherwise beautiful scenery. Vextonar was a funny planet. Everything was artificial, from the paved-over earth to the very air the inhabitants breathed. It had long ago lost its ability to sustain life, but the inhabitants clung to it.

Harrison Goel's cook opened the kitchen door and smiled. "Right on time. Master Goel is in his study. He's on a conference call with several others."

Doris smiled and nodded. "Thank you. I'm a little early."

"I'll make you a sandwich while you wait," Cook

said and started pulling items from one of the huge refrigerators.

"You don't have to do that," Doris said, shuffling her feet. Folks didn't normally welcome an assassin with open arms. *I'm an operative now, not an assassin,* she reminded herself.

Cook smiled as she looked over her shoulder. "You're about to make me very happy, young lady. The least I can do is make you lunch. How's Draif? I haven't seen or heard a thing about that boy in years."

"He's doing well," Doris said, sitting at one of the counters. "He has a mate and seems to be very happy. His father just moved to Charybdis Station too."

Cook's eyes watered. "Oh. That's just about the best thing I've heard in a long time. Draif's mama cared a lot about that man. I always hoped he'd be able to buy Draif, but Master Goel put a high price on him. He didn't want him to go to his father."

Cook set the sandwich in front of Doris, then went back to the counter to continue cutting vegetables. "Now, Master Goel has two sons and one daughter. They're all sitting in on his call, so I'm guessing his fleet finally reached Charybdis Station."

Doris nodded, chewing her food. The contract said to take out all four, Goel and his three children were equally monstrous. The three younger Goels were fully immersed in Humans First.

Cook hummed to herself for a moment. "I suppose Master Goel's youngest brother will inherit. He's a good man and not a bit like the master. Last I heard, he lives on Aruta."

"What about your daughter? Will he let you go to her?"

Cook shook her head, eyes sad. "Kristina passed a few months ago. One of our deliverymen told me."

"I'm sorry," Doris said. "Do you have anyone else?"

"The other slaves and servants are kind enough," Cook said, forcing a smile. "I don't have a bad life."

"What's your name? Draif just called you Cook."

She smiled. "That's all he ever knew me by. When I took over the kitchen, that became my name."

Doris shook her head. "You still have a name. What is it?"

"Gloria," Cook said, voice cracking. "My mother named me Gloria."

Doris's comm chimed, and she read the message. "I can give you five minutes to pack a bag, ma'am. You'll be welcome on Charybdis Station and can leave with me."

Doris would make sure they made room on their ship for the woman. Hell, Juniper would probably hire her on at the diner.

The knife clattered on the counter when Cook dropped it. "Charybdis Station? Me?"

Doris popped the last bit of the sandwich into her mouth and nodded. "Five minutes, Gloria."

Gloria went straight to a door beside the pantry. "I'll be ready."

Doris picked up the dropped knife and grabbed a few others while she was there, then activated her shield, disappearing from sight. She quietly walked past the guards, not bothering with them.

The door to the study had two guards on it, and those she *did* dispatch quickly, using two knifes to slit their throats. After that, she moved fast. Inside, the four people were arguing.

"They're outnumbered," Goel yelled. "We'll have to send another fucking fleet if he fails, Captain Tuggard, and we can't afford it. Order Beldon to surrender. We may be able to ransom our ships. That's how those filthy mercenaries work."

"I'll start working on the funds," the lone woman in the room said, reaching for her tablet. "Charybdis Station must be destroyed. They've made a mockery of us."

Doris quickly tossed one of the knives, and it landed deep in Goel's chest, directly in his heart. Another thrown knife killed the daughter, and Doris drew two more, jumping over a chair to stab the son going for his phaser. The last son wasn't carrying any weapons, but he was running for the door. He was dead in seconds.

Doris stepped over his body and quickly dragged the two dead guards into the room. Then, she deactivated her shield, picked up Goel's comm, and waved at the white-faced captain before setting the comm down on the table so the man had a perfect view of Goel's body.

After taking a few pictures, she activated her shield and left the room. She sent Bendix the images, then deactivated her shield again when she reached the kitchen.

Gloria stood waiting with her bag and twelve other

slaves. Each held a bag of their own.

Doris nodded. They'd make room.

"How will we get off the grounds?" one of the other slaves asked. "They only let us leave one at a time and only if we're running errands."

Doris pointed up toward the sky. Large dark shapes were coming closer to the surface of the planet. "Everyone's about to have a lot more to worry about."

Sheiria

.

SHEIRIA STOOD ON THE BRIDGE OF THE RED SOLACE and watched as Vextonar's planetary defenses activated, firing on the approaching fleets. The Betonize battle cruisers were decimating the pitiful fleet Vextonar had sent to face them as they approached.

Dottie's son and daughter stood with Sheiria, watching their homeworld approach.

"The Vextonar Rebels say they'll have the planetary defenses down in thirty seconds," Sheiria's lieutenant, Javier, said. "Full Moon just messaged. They're finished and will head up to the medical ship once we start our descent."

The leaders of each fleet smiled from their individual screens dotting the left-hand side of the bridge's largest vid-screen.

"Your new covert division is very useful, general," the Fallon general said.

Sheiria nodded. "They are. Any questions before we move to the planet's surface?"

The leaders of each fleet shook their heads.

"We're ready," Admiral Muwali said. The Admiral of the Lost Paw Mercenaries practically vibrated with excitement.

Sheiria couldn't really blame him. It wasn't every day a person got to work with an alliance made of six different mercenary groups and four separate planets.

Ava and the Council filled one of the screens. Ava looked both determined and worried. "Remember, focus on government buildings. We want to reduce civilian casualties as much as possible."

"We'll do what we can, Ava," the Betonize general said. "Hopefully, it will be easier once we get troops on the ground."

"Planetary defenses are down, general," Javier said.

Sheiria smiled. "It's time to do this."

———

Sugarworm System, Planet Rueal

CAS WATCHED HIS CAPTAINS TAKE OUT THE FEW SHIPS Rueal sent to greet the incoming fleets. Draif's contact had told him Humans First were sending everything they had to Charybdis, and it looked like he was right.

All that seemed to be left were the planet's basic military divisions.

The wealthy planet was all but defenseless, and Cas wondered if the planet's government regretted throwing their lot in with HF now.

The leaders of the other fleets accompanying Cas seemed as baffled as he was. They were each visible on the Green Solace's largest vid-screen.

"Why the hell did Rueal's president send all his ships with HF?" the Grellweir general asked.

Cas shrugged. "His head is so far up Malone's ass, he doesn't get much air. That probably makes it hard to think clearly."

"Planetary defenses are down," Crow said through the comm system.

Cas grinned and whooped. "You're the best, Crow."

"I've been waiting on this for a long time," Crow said. "Remove the shit from my planet, so our people can come home."

"With pleasure," the Dedril general said from his screen, smiling. "We're focusing solely on governmental and military buildings. Make sure you get your people to safe zones, Mr. Crow."

The Dedril and Drellian fleets started toward the largest city on the planet while the Siren and Tammolian fleets headed toward the second largest city. Cas and the Cardinal general were responsible for the capital.

"I have people entering the capital now," Crow said. "I'll meet you on the ground."

Cas's pilot flew the Green Solace straight toward

the capital. Malone and Hald were on the planet, but Cas knew Full Moon already had people at Malone's vineyard outside the city. Hald was across the planet, being visited by another Full Moon operative.

"Why aren't the ground defenses firing at us?" Cas's pilot, Yanis, asked. "I expected more resistance from the military forces."

"Uh, Cas," Crow said through the comm. "This may be a lot easier than we planned."

"What is it?"

"Land in front of the Capital building."

"Is there room?"

"They'll make room," Crow said.

Cas looked at his crew and shrugged. "To the Capital building."

By the time they landed and Cas and his crew left the ship, Cas knew what Crow was talking about. A woman stood at the top of the steps of the Capital building. Next to her was the body of the President who had signed over the planet to Malone and Humans First.

"My name is Jada Corvin," the woman said, holding out her hand. "Word came through about thirty minutes ago that Teresa Malone and her cronies are dead. I hope you don't mind, but I and several others joined in your attack. We've wanted Humans First and our incompetent president out of power for a while. We're taking the city now but aren't meeting with much resistance."

Cas shook her hand.

Crow came to stand next to them. "I know Jada. She was a friend of my dad's. She's good people."

Cas grinned. "Nice to meet you, ma'am. If you have things handled here, we'll move on to another city. We have a planet to neutralize."

A few hours from Charybdis Station

DRAIF WATCHED BELDON CORTEZ STARE AT IMAGES OF the bodies of his father, Goel, Malone, and Hald. Several more images appeared. Bendix and Fasi had decided to try to take out as much of Humans First's leadership as possible.

"No," Beldon said, falling into a seat. "That's not possible."

"I wouldn't look for help from Vextonar or Rueal either," General Phillia of Siren's Lament said. "Siren's Lament and Cardinal's Hold are aiding the Green General, Tammol, Aruta, and the Drell in taking control of Rueal. From the updates I'm receiving, it's going rather well."

The Fallon general smiled sweetly. "Fallow and Grellweir are likewise assisting Charybdis Station's Red General, several mercenary groups, and the Betonize president's personal fleet in taking back Vextonar. How foolish of you to leave the planet unprotected."

Fasi gave the man a cold look. "Did you truly think you could continue to devastate the galaxy without consequences? Now, this is the last time I'll ask. Do you surrender?"

Beldon's face turned red and his eyes darted around the bridge of his ship. "We will never surrender!"

Fasi's smile was terrifying. "Good."

The screen went blank, and the HF ships attacked. "Beldon will run," Draif said, moving to the captain's seat.

"I'm on him," Ige said. "My captains know what to do."

Lucas and the others moved to the weapons controls. With the improvements Pops and Tae had made overnight, the Black Heron had a hell of a lot more weaponry than before.

Draif took a breath and focused on the battle around him. Humans First were outnumbered, but that didn't mean they wouldn't do their best to take Charybdis and their allies down with them.

"Ginger, focus on herding those small fighter ships together," Draif said. "General Phillia's fleet is best equipped to fight the battle cruisers, so leave them to her. Lucas and Anders, don't bother with the energy net missiles. Fire the ion missiles instead. I want their shields down. Crimson, Ned, and Alex, man the pulse cannons and aim for those small ships. Use plasma missiles for the larger vessels when we come across them."

Draif watched as his crew worked in tandem with one another. Ginger flew the ship, blocking the movements of several fighter ships, keeping them close together.

Lucas and Anders fired ion missiles into the group and took out the shields of several ships, allowing Crimson and Ned to finish them off with several shots from the pulse cannon.

A mid-grade ship started toward them, and Lucas fired several ion missiles at it, reducing the shields so Alex could take it out with a couple of plasma missiles.

About twenty minutes later, General Pyllia's large ships took out the last battle cruiser, and the remaining HF ships moved from attacking to retreat.

"Finn, don't let any get past your fleet," Fasi ordered. "We finish Humans First today."

"Sure thing, Lord Admiral." Finn's fleet held the line and cut off the retreating ships, destroying them quickly.

Draif watched through the viewport as the last HF ship was torn apart by a plasma missile.

Fasi looked up from his comm. "Audre says they have troops planetside on Vextonar. Winneon and the Prime are fighting hard, but we're gaining ground."

"What about Cas?" Lucas asked.

"They're planetside too, working city to city. The capital is already in our control."

Ige's voice came through the ship's comm. "Draif, it's done. Beldon Cortez's ship is floating rubble."

Draif leaned back in his chair, eyes locking with his mate's. Excitement filled him, and he had to force his body to stay still.

It was over.

21

ANCHORS REST SYSTEM, CHARYBDIS STATION

*L*ucas kept Draif's hand in his as they left the ship. He felt so light and happy, he was practically dancing. "I can't believe it's over. Humans First is really finished."

Draif's eyes narrowed in thought. "There will always be people like them in the galaxy, but hopefully, they'll think twice before committing mass murder."

"Hopefully, no one will ever find another Rising Queen," Fasi said from beside them. "I don't mean to minimize what Humans First did, but that creature plotted and manipulated the lot of them."

Lucas stopped walking when Honey started climbing to the top of his head. For some reason, the little dragon liked to perch up there.

"Grandpa!" Rizzie's voice interrupted their conversation. The little Siren ran up the ship's ramp and jumped into Fasi's arms.

Sami followed with Pax. The little boy hugged Draif's legs. "Are the bad guys gone now?"

Lucas grinned. "They most certainly are, Sami boy."

Draif's father and stepmom waited at the bottom of the ramp with the rest of the neighborhood and most of Full Moon.

Leander gave them a worried look. "Is everyone alright?"

"We're fine." Lucas patted his shoulder. "The ship took a few hits, but Tae will have her all fixed up in no time."

"Sure will," Tae said, grinning. "I can't believe I'm the engineer on the Lord Admiral and Vice Admiral's flagship."

Leander grinned. "I can't believe I'm the father of the Vice Admiral of Charybdis Station."

Tempest gently shoved Draif's shoulder. "Way to set the bar high, big brother."

Lucas grabbed her in a hug, and Honey struggled to keep her balance. "It's not a competition, Tempest. If it was, we'd all lose."

"Speak for yourself, Lucas." Renee strode toward the ship, Milo in her arms. "I can still outfight him. For now."

Fasi set Rizzie down just in time to get an armful of his wife and grandson. "Humans First is over."

Renee tucked her head into his chest. "Good. I don't like being left behind."

Lucas recognized a pair of gray eyes over the sea of people gathering at the ship. "Ige! Over here."

Draif's friend pushed through people to get to them. "I left some ships on cleanup duty, but thank you for letting us dock, Lord Admiral. I'm glad this is over."

Fasi nodded. "You and your people are welcome here anytime, Mr. Ige. You put yourself at great risk to keep us updated on HF's movements."

Lucas gripped the human's shoulder and squeezed. "I appreciate you making sure Beldon Cortez didn't get away."

"I can't believe he ran," Ginger said, scowling. "What kind of leader orders his people to attack, then runs?"

"A shitty one," Draif answered dryly, before turning to Fasi. "Lucas and I will check in with medical and get a number on the dead and wounded."

"Good. I'll get the Council together, and we'll address the station." Fasi grinned. "Look at you, Draify, stepping right into your role."

Draif groaned. "Don't call me Draify. It's embarrassing."

"Draify loo," Ma said, pulling Draif into a big hug. "Love isn't embarrassing, baby boy."

Lucas snickered, and Draif gave him a dark look. "Sorry, Ma. The Vice Admiral and I have to get to work."

Ma set Draif down and leaned over to kiss Lucas's cheek. "Come to Leti's house when you're done. We have celebrating to do."

Pops wrapped an arm around Ige's shoulder. "Mr. Ige, you're coming with us. Gus is already at the house, and he wants to talk to you about your shipping business. He and I got to talking about the access control systems on your ships."

Draif took Lucas's hand again, then looked hesitant.

"Wait. Should I hold your hand? It's not very professional."

Lucas tugged him toward the docked medical ship. "Love, nothing and no one will keep me from holding your hand. People can deal with it."

———

A FEW HOURS LATER, THEY MADE IT BACK TO THEIR neighborhood. The streets were full of very happy people. Lucas saw soldiers from all six planets in the Anchor's Rest System as well as Ige's fleet.

Councilman Delino had his arm around Becca as he moved from group to group, laughing and talking. Lucas noticed all of the Council mixed in with captains, generals, and civilians.

"Think we can make it to Leti's house?" Draif leaned into his side, and Lucas stopped walking and closed his eyes. "What's wrong, Lucas?"

He opened his eyes and met Draif's gaze. "The Queen is dead, and Humans First is destroyed. Most importantly of all, you're my mate. I'm at your side, Draif, and I always will be. I'm sorry. It all is just sinking in."

Draif smiled. "I know what you mean."

Gus ran up to them. "There you two are. Ma and Sybil have food on tables in the backyard, and I think someone snuck another goat in there too."

Lucas tilted his head, and Honey slid to his shoulder. "Another goat?"

Gus's face scrunched up. "Yeah. There's a long-haired black and white Havenite goat with these huge ears in the yard with Wobbles and Trixie."

Draif snorted. "Who brings a goat to a celebration?"

Lucas grinned. "The Havenites. They heard Leti likes animals."

"Hack is going to be so mad," Draif said, laughing. "Leti will accept the goat into his family and pamper and love it."

Gus winced. "You should go tell Renee that. I think she was wondering about making the goat dinner. She really doesn't want more pets to take care of."

"Uh oh." Draif let go of Lucas's hand and ran toward Leti's house.

Lucas took his time getting to the house. He didn't want to get between Draif and Renee. "Gus, how is your family settling in?"

The young man grinned. "They're good. We've never had such a nice place to live in before, and Mom is happy I'm more legit."

"You're alright with working for Charybdis Station instead of freelancing?"

"It's different, but honestly, it's even more challenging. There's a lot I can do for Charybdis Station, and it gives my family a solid and stable home."

They made it to the house, and Lucas laughed. Draif and Renee were feeding apple slices to the goat. It was bigger than Trixie but looked a lot more placid. Its hair was shiny and well-kept, and Lucas suspected it might be a little high maintenance. Rizzie and Ava were brushing it, and there were several bows in its hair.

"Yeah. No one's eating that goat," Lucas said.

Later that night, after the numbers were reported, the goat was welcomed into the family, and the drinking was done, Lucas finally had his mate to himself. Honey, Chutney, and Marmalade were curled together on the master bedroom's window seat, and Ige slept in a guestroom down the hall.

Draif straddled Lucas, face pressed into his neck. "I can't believe it worked. I've been planning for months, but so many things could have gone wrong."

Lucas thought of the images of the big four's bodies. "Your backup plans had backup plans, love. I'm not at all surprised we won. No one is. You, Fasi, Ava, and the Council made sure we were as prepared as possible. Fuck, I didn't realize it, but they even had Burnished ships out there. They were manned by Havenites *and* Burnished, but still. That was Burnished Outpost's first real space battle."

"Thank Ava for that. The woman has a way of making allies."

Lucas smiled into Draif's hair and thought of the very brief conversation he'd managed to have with Fasi about Ava. "She certainly does."

Draif leaned back, giving Lucas a stricken look. "Goel and Beldon have been hanging over my head for years. Now they're gone, and there's this emptiness in my gut. I didn't realize I was clinging so hard to my past."

Lucas pushed a strand of hair from Draif's face. "Now, we can plan for the future."

Draif bit his lip. "It doesn't feel like it's over. It doesn't feel like it's real."

"I don't think it will until Hack and the others get back," Lucas said, stroking Draif's back. "I love you, Draif Ando. You are the most stubborn, persistent, and intelligent man I know. I am in awe of you every day and so thankful you're my mate. I don't know why the fates would think I was worthy of you, but fuck it, I'm going to take it."

"I love you too. It's... You're Lucas. You're everything."

Lucas stretched his arm and tried to reach the drawer of his side table. "Give me a second. I can... almost... reach it. *Ha!* Got it." He held a ring out to Draif. "This was my dad's wedding ring. My mom's was very feminine, but if you'd rather wear it, that's good too. We're getting married, right? I mean, you love me, I love you, so what else is there?"

Draif buried his face in his hand. "The romance is killing me."

Lucas shrugged, grinning. "What do you say?"

Draif cupped his face and kissed him, lips warm and firm. "I say, fuck yes. I'll wear your dad's ring, and we can rework your mom's to suit you or get you a new one. Whatever you want."

Lucas gave him a smug look. "Proposal done. Look at that."

"You have such a way with words," Draif said dryly.

"Hey now, you're the one that writes poems about me."

"That's art, so it's different."

2 2

Two weeks later, Draif stood in the spaceport with Moses, Renee, and Fasi. They were surrounded by Leti's kids. Lucas stood with Nessa, the little girl bouncing in place, excited to finally meet her new mother.

Sybil and Tempest were back at Leti's house, cooking a huge welcome home meal. Draif's family was looking forward to meeting Leti.

The Blue Solace and the rest of Hack's fleet finally docked, and the doors to the cargo holds opened. Leti's brood moved as one. "Daddies!"

Rizzie carried Milo and led the way to Leti and Hack. Draif had to fight tears when his friend started sobbing and hugging his children. Mo, Alex, and Rose surrounded Hack, and the general disappeared in his siblings' arms. The two groups quickly merged into a pile of arms and tears. Renee sniffled, then pulled Moses and Fasi forward and into the hug too.

Leti's newest addition, Elril, stood to the side, shy

and nervous.

Rizzie's head popped out of the tangled mess of a hug. "Elril. Come hug us. Brothers hug their sisters, damn it."

Elril grinned and ran to them, and Rizzie and Sami pulled him into the pile.

Hack's dog, Gravy, and Alois's dog, Peri, took advantage of the chaos to find some privacy behind a few stacked crates. Draif winced and looked away. There might be more puppies soon.

He looked up and noticed Wyatt and Morgan with the twins and Estella. Wyatt's mom and stepdad waited their turn for hugs. Next to them, a well-rested and healthy-looking Sebastian showed Mordy to his sisters, Sai and Salla, while Alois held Nina in his arms, swaying and cooing to the baby.

Closer to the ship, Selene had Xu in her arms, and Draif could read the woman well enough to know she was close to tears. Nettle and Lilah hugged, their daughter Sophie between them, and Dannol knelt in front of Nessa, talking quickly before hugging his daughter.

Dru, Lerais, and Juniper greeted Finn, and Draif smiled when he saw his crew crowded around Moyra and Olla.

"Damn." Draif rushed to the ramp when he saw Beck helping Beol walk. The pregnant man was massive. "Beol, are you about to give birth?"

The former assassin glared at him. "Fuck you, Vice Admiral. I'm carrying gods damned twins, and I'm slow."

Grumpy kitty, Draif thought.

Ma and Beck's sisters surrounded Beol and whisked him away in a circle of chatter, fussing, and promises of foot and back rubs.

Beck stood there, blinking. "What just happened?"

Pops grinned and hugged his son. "Your mate needed some loving, son. It's good to see you back. Where's my Icarus?"

Beck's Bracken son came from the ship. He carried Beck's Crell daughter, Aketil.

"My grandbabies." Pops pushed Beck aside and ran to Icarus and Aketil.

Beck sighed. "I feel unloved."

Draif laughed and gave the big Grell a hug. "You're still loved, big guy. I'm glad you all made it back."

"Me too." Beck grinned. "I hear we missed out on seeing Humans First get crushed."

Draif smirked. "Their fleets are destroyed, their leaders dead, and Cas and Sheiria are in the last stages of taking control of Vextonar and Rueal, HF's largest supporters."

"Good job, Vice Admiral," Beck said, slapping Draif's back.

Draif grinned, then noticed something interesting. "Look there."

Draif and Beck watched Val approach Death, face uncertain and almost tortured. Death didn't say anything. He just pulled the large Betonize man into his arms and kissed him.

"Well," Beck said, brows raised. "Fire was right."

"I told you so," Fire said from behind him. "I see

them together all the time. I think Death loves Val." The Element had his two guinea pigs on his shoulders and a cinnamon stick in his mouth. "Aren't they cute?"

Draif snorted. "I'm sure they'd appreciate that description."

Beck laughed. "Yeah."

Fire bounced and turned in circles. "Look. There's Meggie. She thinks she looks scary so she's trying to sneak past Nessa. Dannol thinks it's a stupid plan, but he doesn't want her to feel bad."

Draif frowned and spun around. Nessa had been looking forward to seeing Meggie. There would be no damn sneaking.

Sax helped her friend walk along the edges of the crowds while Gregor carried their bags, hovering close behind the women. Meggie was draped in a long, thick coat with the hood pulled up, hiding her face.

Draif whistled to Lucas, and his mate turned to him. Draif nodded at Meggie, and Lucas's face turned dark. He tapped Nessa and Dannol on the shoulders and pointed toward Meggie.

Nessa's face lit up. "Mama!" She pulled out of Dannol's arms and ran toward Meggie.

The gathered crowd grew quiet and watched the little girl.

Meggie yelped and pushed behind Sax. "Don't look, Nessa. I'm hideous, and I don't want to scare you."

Nessa ignored her and pushed Sax aside. She pulled Meggie's hood back, and Draif's heart about broke. Meggie had no hair and no real facial features. Her metal frame and the bare start to her wired musculature was in place, but she had no lips, no skin, and no ears.

Nessa didn't care, she hugged her, tears falling. "Mama, you're here. Hug me!"

Meggie gasped, then did as she was told.

"Meggie girl, why are you hiding?" Becca and the ever-present Delino joined them. "You're my beautiful, heroic girl."

"Mom," Meggie said, voice strained. She held an arm out, and Becca joined them. "You really don't mind my face, Nessa?"

Nessa looked puzzled. "You got hurt saving everyone. Scars are part of us. I showed you mine when we talked on the vid-screen, remember?"

Fasi and the rest of the Council approached them. "Meggie, welcome home. We are honored you've chosen to become a Charybdis Station citizen. Please don't hide away from us."

The crowds drew closer and started to cheer when they recognized Meggie. Draif wiped his eyes. They had seen Meggie's actions and not a damn person was concerned about her appearance. They were just happy she was alive.

———

DRAIF SAT WITH LUCAS IN ONE OF THE COMFORTABLE lounge chairs in the backyard. He held Aketil in his arms, transfixed by the Crell baby's black eyes. Her tiny fist gripped one of his fingers, and she squeezed.

Ige and Gus sat nearby, heads close together as they

talked about Ige's ships. Draif had a feeling Ige would be making Charybdis Station a frequent stop in the future. He liked it here and got along well with everyone.

Ginger and Olla sat together on the ground next to Draif's chair. The two women whispered to one another, occasionally darting a look his way. Leander stood behind them, examining one of the large trees in the yard.

"I can't believe Beck adopted a Crell baby." Lucas nuzzled the back of Draif's neck, and he shuddered.

"I can."

Draif fought back the longing that suddenly filled him. Lucas and he didn't have time for a baby right now. Over the past couple of weeks, Draif had started taking on responsibilities as the Vice Admiral. He had an office next to Fasi's and a full schedule. He even had an assistant.

Aketil gurgled and squeezed Draif's finger again. "Lucas, can we have a baby?"

Lucas choked on air and started coughing.

"Whoa there, Lucas. Are you alright?" Leander patted Lucas on the back.

Draif flushed. They really didn't have time for children. Really. Life was too busy.

"Thanks, Leander," Lucas finally managed to say. "Draif and I are gonna have kids. I'll have to do some work in the house and pass on more of my duties to Anders. Should we get a dog? It seems like Leti told me every kid should have a dog."

Leander blinked. "Draif is pregnant?"

Draif started laughing, joy filling him. "No, Dad. I'm not pregnant. Yet."

Leti sat on the arm of the chair, patting Draif's cheek. "Did you say you're pregnant? Already?"

Draif gave him an incredulous look. "You're the one that got pregnant just days after meeting your mate, so no judging. Besides, I'm not pregnant."

Meggie wandered over with Nessa. She reached out and pricked him with one of her fingers, collecting a drop of his blood. "I'll go ask Mom to test your blood. She carries her scanner with her all the time. I'll help Sybil make up a nutritional menu for you. Another week from now, and I could scan you myself."

Draif groaned. "I'm not pregnant yet!"

Meggie ignored him and ran to Becca. Draif couldn't help but be happy the annoying woman didn't seem a bit self-conscious about her appearance anymore.

Lucas buried his face against Draif's shoulder, body shaking with laughter.

"If you're pregnant, I'm getting your kid a damn pet," Reed said, sitting in a chair nearby. "I still owe you for giving Herma her damn Gelross."

"Gelross?" Leti gasped. "I don't have a Gelross."

"You have another goat." Lucas pointed at Muffin, the newest addition to Leti's family. The silky-haired goat was covered in bows. He stood with Wobble and Trixie at the largest flower bush in the backyard.

"Isn't he the prettiest goat in the galaxy?" Leti sighed happily, chin resting on his fist.

Leander sniffled. "Draif. A few minutes ago, you called me Dad. Did you notice that?"

Draif smiled softly. "I've been calling you Dad in my head for a while now."

A pack of children ran by, filling the air with loud laughter and squeals. Elril was right in the middle of them, smiling and happy. The sandbox was full of the smaller children, and Princess Buttercup lounged beside it with Mo's jackrabbit, Abbot. Stardust and Honey perched on the big dragon's back while Aagy grumbled as he gently chewed on Princess's tail.

"I think Princess just became a dad," Leander said, eyes sparkling. "Watch him with Aagy."

Princess turned slowly, rumbling. Aagy let go of his tail and whined, eyes big and contrite. The younger dragon snuggled up against Princess's side.

"Aww." Draif wondered why his eyes were watering. *Fucking dragons and their cuteness.*

"Speaking of babies, I think Gravy and Periwinkle are going to be parents again soon. I caught them going at it at the spaceport." Leti winced. "I haven't told Will yet."

"You should definitely give Draif one of those puppies," Reed said, sipping his ale. "I think he'd really like that."

Draif glared at Reed. "Why did I decide I like you?"

Leander gasped. "Draif, who is that man standing with Tempest?"

Draif looked to where his father pointed. Juniper stood in front of Tempest with an odd look of wonder in his eyes. His golden skin was darkened in a flush, and he looked almost shy. Tempest, on the other hand, looked utterly bemused.

"That's Juniper. Lucas, would you happen to know how Fallon find their mates?"

Lucas grinned. "Ava told me that when a Fallon meets their mate, they see an aura around the person."

Leti's face lit up with excitement. "Do you think Juniper and Tempest are life mates?"

Leander frowned. "Juniper better be a good person. I don't like the way he's looking at my little girl."

"He's one of the best people I know, Dad." Draif waved at Tempest, gesturing for her to come over. She blinked in confusion but moved away from Juniper. Draif's friend followed her, moving as if there were a string attaching him to Tempest.

"Draif? This guy says he's a friend of yours." Tempest blushed. "He also says he's my life mate."

Leander sighed. "Wello discover their life mates at sight. Are you drawn to him, Tempest?"

Juniper gave her a hopeful look, and she blushed again. "Yeah."

"I can vouch for him," Draif said, again blinking away tears. *Fucking sisters and their cuteness.*

Tempest frowned. "Wait. Aren't you my boss? The one that's been away on a mission?"

"Yes," Juniper said, nodding. "I'm sorry. If you don't want to be with me, I won't hold it against you. You'll always have a job at my diner."

She bit her lip. "I never said I didn't want to be with you."

Fasi's voice carried across the yard, interrupting

them. "Can I have everyone's attention?"

Juniper sent the man a scowl, but the large crowd quieted down, turning its attention to Fasi. Leti had invited the Council and several of the other Anchors Rest military leaders that were still on the station.

"While so many of you are gathered here, I thought it might be a good time to take the last step in our journey with the Rising Queen."

Sebastian stepped up and held out the Queen's artifact. When Meggie had defeated the Queen, her soul had been freed from the host. Death had held her soul while another Shaman cleansed it. However, he couldn't hold it forever, and it was bound to the artifact.

Dr. Orsla Manning came forward and held up a tray. On it, were the remains of three artifacts. "The Rising Queen's three Elements Air, Water, and Life were killed by Charybdis Station. When their essences retreated to their artifacts, we were faced with a dilemma."

Delino cleared his throat. "The Council thought about trying to use the Elements to our advantage, but ultimately agreed with our Lord Admiral that they were too dangerous. Dr. Manning, Dr. Verion Morrick, and Dr. Wyatt Morrick worked with our own Charybdis Station historian Leti and shaman Sebastian to devise a way to destroy the artifacts and end this cycle of pain and death."

"It took a good while to create a device capable of destroying the artifacts," Dr. Manning said. "However, we did it, and we have managed to destroy Air, Water, and Life's artifacts after disintegrating their essences. Here are all that remains of them. These Elements can no longer be raised to wreak destruction on our galaxy."

Everyone cheered, and Draif patted Leti's knee. "You're our Charybdis Station historian, huh?"

Leti beamed. "Fasi said we could have one of the older barracks to turn into a small liberal arts university. Advaith and some of the other professors from Vextonar are going to stay here and help me get it established."

Ige leaned closer. "Are you going to teach Shamanism?"

Leti blinked. "Uh, I don't know if Sebastian will go for that. Chocolate squirrels, I don't even know if that's a good idea. Damn it, Chad. Now it's in my head."

Ige grinned. "Not sorry."

"Our last step," Fasi said, drawing their attention back, "is to destroy the Queen's artifact, so her soul can finally be free to rest in peace, cleansed of the evil that tainted her for so long."

Dr. Manning set aside the broken artifacts and pulled out a solid black box. "This box is the nifty piece of tech we created. It's truly a mix of Crellic Shamanism and technology. It uses the extremes of all Elements at once to break the artifact."

She set it on the table, and Sebastian stepped up. "The Queen wasn't always evil. During her natural lifetime, she brought peace to her people, had a mate, and tried her best to have a happy life. She was brave and kind. It's time she had the rest she deserves."

He set the artifact inside the box, closed it, then stepped back.

Dr. Manning pressed something on her tablet, and the box rose, hovering over the table. It lit up, the black glass almost transparent. Each of the flat sides of the box had an etched symbol on it. Draif assumed it was one for each Element.

The first side lit up, and the box shook for a few moments, then stilled. The next side lit up, and the box shook again. Each side took its turn until the box finally stilled and slowly lowered back to the table.

Sebastian opened the top and stepped back, gasping. A beautiful green, brown, and gold wisp floated out of the box. The colors swirled together rich and healthy.

"The Queen's soul," Draif whispered.

Death and Fire stepped forward, tears filling their eyes. "My Queen?"

The wisp danced around them, and Draif could almost hear a tinkling laughter. "I wonder what she's saying."

Sebastian grinned. "For those of you who can't hear her, the Queen is telling her two friends to thank us for freeing her and stopping the destruction her people inadvertently started. She says she will be more than happy to rest but only when her beloved does. She plans to go to Earth and stay with him for the rest of his life cycle."

Leti leaned into Draif's side, almost sitting on top of Lucas too. He set his head on Draif's shoulder and wiped his eyes. "They can't touch each other. Won't that be a living hell?"

Draif met Lucas's eyes. "No. They're together. Touch is great – in fact, it's fucking amazing – but it's not the most important thing. I would want to be with Lucas no matter what the situation was. I can understand why the Queen would want to go to Earth."

The wisp slowly disappeared, and the quiet backyard erupted in chatter. Fasi held his hands up again, eyes wet. "Okay, okay. Settle down. I have a few announcements to make before we get back to eating, drinking, and making merry. First, the seven planets – or in our case, station – in the Anchors Rest System have finally decided on a leader for the Anchors Rest Defense Force."

Ava stood and moved to stand beside him, practically bouncing in excitement.

"Our own Ava Dallinghart has agreed to accept the position as Commander of the ARDF." Fasi laughed when everyone started cheering again. "We love Ava, and she is a fair-minded, intelligent woman who is on good terms with every planet in the system. She was essential in gaining the allies we needed to neutralize Vextonar and Rueal. Even though I hate to lose her, I can think of no one better suited to this position."

Ava waved and walked back to her seat next to Cordelia and Quinn.

"The second announcement I have is Charybdis Station's plan to offer aid to each of the planets that were devastated by HF. My son and our Green General, Caspian Juren, will be leading a fleet of volunteers from the Anchors Rest System to each of the planets. His lieutenant will fill in while he is gone."

Leti clapped loudly with everyone else. "That is perfect. We haven't been able to do much since we've been focusing on the Queen and HF."

Fasi cleared his throat. "An anonymous donor handed over a large fortune to help in the aid. This money was taken straight from HF's now deceased leadership."

Draif shot Gus a look, but his friend just smiled innocently.

"One more announcement," Fasi said. "Then you can all get back to the fun. When Vextonar allied themselves with HF, they sold many of their citizens into slavery. I can't abide by that. Charybdis Station's Blue Lieutenant will lead a small fleet of ships to find and rescue these people. We'll offer our aid as needed, but Finn will be leaving for Rueal in two weeks. We'll bring them home and hopefully reunite them with their families."

The backyard filled with cheers again, and Fasi laughed as he sat back down beside Renee, taking Pepper from her.

"Well," Leti said. "That's a lot of work he just gave everyone."

"You have a university to establish," Draif said, nudging his friend. "Ava, Cas, and Finn can handle their tasks. We'll be here if they need us."

"Captain," Olla said, leaning over. "Moyra's captaining a ship in Finn's fleet. She needs a pilot."

Draif arched a brow. "It's a permanent position,

isn't it?"

Olla gave him a guilty look. "Yeah."

He gave Ginger a considering look. "Well, Ginger. Will you be the Black Heron's pilot?"

Ginger smiled and fluttered her lashes. "If you insist."

"Draif," Meggie said, interrupting them. She pulled Sybil behind her. "The blood test shows you *are* pregnant, and you need more vitamins in your diet. When Beck, Gregor, and Mom get me repaired, I'll scan you and let you know the gender and species of your baby, but Sybil will work with Lucas to change up your meal plans."

Leti squealed and hugged him, while Lucas sat frozen, arms still wrapped around Draif. "We're having a baby?" Lucas asked. "Really?"

Meggie groaned. "Do I need to repeat myself? I have a little girl to cuddle with."

Sybil chuckled. "Go on, Meggie. I'll talk them through their shock."

Draif leaned back into his mate's arms, pulling his best friend with him. He could see the future before him. He'd work hard to make the station even better than it already was, then go home to Lucas and their children.

Leti would be right next door, and they'd visit one another all the time. His dad, stepmom, and siblings would be right down the road, and the rest of his family and friends nearby.

For once in his life, he looked forward to the future. *His* future.

Draif held Lucas's hand as they watched the large but simple wedding ceremony in the center garden of Full Moon's neighborhood. Beol had given birth to the twins last week and had insisted on marrying Beck as soon as possible. No one was going to tell the new father *no*. Not when his grumpiness had increased tenfold.

Finn and a few of the others were on a portable vid-screen at the back of the guests, watching. Wyther, Yeardley, and the other volunteers were finally back from Rueal. HF had been completely eradicated from the planet. The strange-looking toad Fyrling sat in Yeardley's lap. Coni had told him that her Mom loved Mr. Toad and completely spoiled him.

Nessa sat next to Coni, and Dannol and Meggie were nearby. Charybdis Station's hero was back to her old, stylish self. Her two Bracken friends, Sax and Icarus, were officially a couple and had a newly adopted daughter. The little girl was one of the rescued children from Genarg, and she seemed quite happy with her new parents.

The rest of their friends and family spread out in the garden too. Draif tried hard not to notice Juniper and Tempest snuggled up together nearby. Having a sister was an odd thing. He wanted to both pulverize Juniper and thank him for making Tempest smile. *Odd.*

Draif settled his head on Lucas's shoulder, then pulled his mate's tail around to play with it. Every part of his mate was fascinating to him. He didn't think he'd ever get tired of hearing his voice or touching his skin.

"Love, the wedding's over," Lucas whispered. "Can I have my tail back?"

"No." Draif pouted. "I want it."

Fasi dropped onto the ground next to him. "So, did you talk to Finn?"

"Honey, we're at a wedding," Renee complained. She carried Milo with her. "Leave him alone."

Draif grinned. "I did talk to him. He arrived on Rueal yesterday. Crow is going to meet with him later today, and they'll go to Malone's estate to start looking for information."

"Good," Fasi said, leaning back on his hands.

Sami ran over and jumped on Fasi. "Grandpa, I saw Mr. Death kissing Val behind the big tree."

Draif grinned and eyed Death. His clothes were askew, and he was blushing as Fire loudly announced to the crowds that Val was Death's life mate.

Renee sighed. "That poor man gets no privacy."

"I'm glad Val and he are staying," Fasi said. "I was

afraid he'd leave and go back to Frost Veil to set up house. It would upset Wyatt and Morgan if he left."

Renee arched an eyebrow. "It wouldn't upset you?"

Fasi shrugged, giving them a sheepish look. "Okay, okay. I like the man."

Draif leaned up and kissed his mate, content to enjoy the beautiful day and listen to the chatter around them.

ALSO BY C.W. GRAY

The Blue Solace Series – science fiction/fantasy, mpreg

1. The Mercenary's Mate – https://amzn.to/2MAOFEH
2. The General's Mate – https://amzn.to/2G1abRE
3. The Soldier's Mate – https://amzn.to/2S7R6ng
4. The Lieutenant's Mate – https://amzn.to/2THZ47w
5. The Engineer's Mate – https://amzn.to/2HpI4vH
6. The Captain's Mate –
7. The Rebel's Mate – *Coming Soon*

*More sci-fi spin-off series from the Blue Solace book world
will be coming soon.

The Hobson Hills Omegas – non-shifter, mpreg, omega
verse

1. Falling for the Omega – https://amzn.to/2BgWURV
2. Snow Kisses for My Omega – https://amzn.to/2TdDiol
3. Romancing the Omega – https://amzn.to/2UNENKD

4. Healing the Omega – https://amzn.to/2FNcXrY
5. A Pint for my Omega – https://amzn.to/2XItQf7
6. Unraveling the Omega – https://amzn.to/2xRCnRL
7. The Alpha's Christmas Wish – https://amzn.to/2qXkGAl
8. Noah's story (Title to be determined) – *Coming Soon*

Hobson Hills Shorts – short stories from the world of Hobson Hills Omegas

1. The Beta's Love Song – https://amzn.to/2UrRPNN
2. Bennett's Dream – https://amzn.to/2GwSpG3
3. Justin's Journey – https://amzn.to/2DhW1t1
4. Grey's Gift – https://amzn.to/2BcjxXf
5. Hobson Hills Shorts: Volume One – https://amzn.to/2M3oGGZ

Holiday Omegas Shorts – holiday short stories from the world of The Silver Isles – paranormal, mpeg

1. Cauldron Cake Pops and a Witch's Kiss – https://amzn.to/33wMrhc
2. Sugar Cookies and a Witch's Love – https://amzn.to/2NE4CeJ
3. Candy Hearts and a Witch's Ring – *Coming in*

February, 2020

The Silver Isles – paranormal, mermen, mpreg

1. The Guppy Prince – https://
    amzn.to/2q9Q8en
2. The Not so Little Merman – *Coming Soon*
3. The Sea Witch – *Coming Soon*

If you would like to keep up with releases, please like and follow me on Instagram (@c.w._gray) or Facebook (@cwgrayauthor), join C.W. Gray's Reading Nook on Facebook, or visit my website at cwgrayauthor.com

Excerpt from *The Rebel's Mate* – book seven in The Blue Solace

Aiden Crow rode a speeder through the near empty street of Pagent's Distillery. The city had been one of the last HF controlled cities to holdout against the rebellion. The Jevio family had unofficially controlled the profitable city for generations and they refused to give up that power.

As he turned into one of the darkened neighborhoods in the city, Parker's voice came through the comm in Crow's helmet. "Michael Jevio just surrendered, boss." Crow's second in command was leading the attack at the Jevio mansion. "Old man Jevio isn't there, but we got the rest of the family."

"Good." Crow's voice was too gruff even to his own ears. "The government building just fell to Jada's soldiers."

"What went wrong?" Parker asked, voice solemn.

Damn asshole can read me too well. Crow zoomed through an empty shopping center, ignoring the burning garbage and bloodstained cement. "We lost more people than usual. City enforcement sided with Jevio's people and the fucking Belcrest Assassins showed up in force."

"Who did we lose?" Parker asked quietly.

"Horski and Mel." They had lost more, but those two had been Crow's people. Two people that Crow had dragged into this stinking pile of dog shit.

"Damn it," Parker cursed. The Dedril was quiet a moment. "Don't let this fuck with your head, boss. They knew what they were doing."

"Horski's wife wasn't so forgiving." Crow gritted his teeth as he drove past abandoned houses. He felt the eyes watching him from the dark and a shiver ran down his back.

"You talked to her by yourself?" Parker cursed again. "Boss, that was stupid."

Crow drove past a familiar dilapidated office building. The security stations around the building were burning, smoke billowing from them. *Dad, you would hate to see it now. This place was your pride and joy.*

He shook his head and focused on the present. "I didn't want to wait. Mel's parents took it better. I'll make arrangements."

"I'll get Staci on it." Parker sighed. "Come home, boss. We'll drink to our friends."

"One more stop." Crow parked in front of a large, darkened house. The neighborhood had been an old and respected one before HF and the fighting. Now, it was almost as derelict as his dad's old office building.

"Tell your mom I said hello," Parker said wryly, then disconnected.

Coming Soon...

Excerpt from *Falling for the Omega*– Book One in the Hobson Hills Omegas Series

Carter loaded the last of his tools into his new work van and shut the door. His first day in his new profession was off to a good start. He had three clients to see today and eight spread out during the rest of the week.

Finally getting his plumbing license had been a good idea, even if his perfect, wealthy family hated the idea of him being a plumber.

Hell, they had also hated the idea of him being a soldier and of him moving out of state when he came back injured. They pretty much hated every decision he made.

The crisp fall wind was cold, but the gold, brown, and red leaves on the trees and ground made the cold worth dealing with. Autumn in Maine sure wasn't the same as autumn in Georgia, but so far, he was damn happy with the move. There was a peace here amongst the trees that he hadn't managed to find anywhere else.

"Hi, Mr. Neighbor!"

A child's voice came from behind him, startling Carter. He spun around, stumbling a bit on his prosthesis, and faced the little girl standing a few feet from his van.

She looked about five or six, with two black braids, caramel skin, and a freckled nose. When she smiled brightly, he saw a small gap between her two front teeth.

A black and gray miniature schnauzer sat at her feet, gaze stern and trained on him.

He looked around and didn't see any adults. His little half acre tract was quite a ways back from the road, nestled between a good-sized apple orchard on one side and a thick forest on the other.

Where the hell had this little girl come from?

"My name's Olive, and I brought you a welcome basket. I made it myself, but Daddy made you one too. He's gonna bring it tonight. I wanted you to get mine first, 'cause it's from me and then we'll be best friends." The little girl paused to take a breath. Her wide brown eyes sparkled and met his straight on, innocent and fearless. "We'll be best friends forever."

She didn't even seem to see the scars along the side of his face. The burn marks had already made two kids cry at the grocery store yesterday. Both times, the parents had been too embarrassed to apologize. They just grabbed their kids and ran.

"Uh, where's your daddy, Olive?" His voice was

deep and cracked, broken by the scarring on his neck. Her adoring stare was starting to freak him out a little. He'd never really been around kids.

"He's at home," she answered and handed him the basket. "See what I brought you? Look, look, look."

"Do you know your phone number? Maybe we could give your daddy a call," Carter said, taking the basket from Olive. He pulled the small hand towel from the top and almost dropped the basket. "Is that a hedgehog?"

"Yep! That's Hodges the hedgehog. He wanted to come visit too. Oh and this is Winston," she said and knelt to pet the small dog.

"Okay, your number?" He tried to keep his gruff voice kind. No sense in scaring the kid.

"Olive! Olive Persephone Wilson! Where are you?" A man's voice called from the orchard, full of panic and desperation.

"Uh oh," Olive said. She hurriedly looked around, then darted behind his van, Winston following her. "That's Daddy." She poked her head out and stared hard. "Tell. Him. Nothing."

She quickly hid again when a young omega rushed out of the orchard. He was her father, had to be. He looked just like her.

Carter suddenly couldn't catch his breath. The man in front of him was simply adorable. He was short and well formed, a little chubby. His black hair fell in curls around his face, and his wide hazel eyes contrasted beautifully with his caramel skin. The same freckles that decorated his daughter's nose, fell across his own.

Where it looked cute on the kid, on her father... Bad thoughts, Carter! Bad thoughts!

"Have you seen a little girl? Black hair? Brown eyes? Miniature schnauzer with her? Maybe a hedgehog?"

Carter stared at the handsome man, mouth gaping, for too long.

The man frowned at him, tilting his head. "Are you alright?" His shy smile revealed the small gap between his front teeth.

Oh fuck, he was so damn perfect. He met Carter's eyes too, didn't even glance at the scars.

"Mister?"

Carter shook his head and did his best to pull himself together. He smiled, as best he could with the scar tissue, and nodded toward the van, holding a finger to his lips, encouraging the man to keep quiet.

Olive's father rolled his eyes and stomped around the van. A squealing Olive ran from her hiding spot and hid behind Carter, hugging him around the waist.

"Mr. Neighbor, save me!" Her giggling told him she wasn't too worried about her father catching her.

"Olive, you scared me to death running off like that." Her father really did look worried. "What have I told you about leaving the house without me?"

"But daddy," she whined. "I wanted to meet Mr. Neighbor. We're best friends now, and I gave him a welcome basket. I was being hospital."

Carter frowned. Hospital?

"Hospitable, baby girl, and it doesn't matter. You are too little to be wandering around by yourself and talking to strangers. No television time this week, and you have to clean out Pooka and Banjo's stalls on Saturday."

Olive gave a big sigh and leaned her forehead into Carter's leg. "Okay, Daddy, but it was worth it. I have a new best friend now."

The man met Carter's stare, a question in his eyes. Carter nodded and gave his best half smile.

"Well, maybe our new neighbor would like to come over for dinner one night? So that we can meet him properly," the man said.

"Yay! Mr. Neighbor, can you come tonight? Daddy's gonna make apple dumplins for dessert."

Carter smiled at the little girl and nodded. "Yeah, if it's okay with your dad."

The man smiled and nodded eagerly. "That would be great. I hardly ever get to cook for anyone but Olive." He gave a flustered look and held out his hand. "Oh, I forgot. My name is Elijah Wilson. I live in the farmhouse with the orchard. Of course, you've met Olive."

Carter shook his hand, touch lingering longer than it should. He was reluctant to release him but finally did. "Yeah, I'm Carter Benson. Just moved here from Georgia."

"Wow, so Maine's probably a bit different, huh?"

"Yeah, but all the colors on the trees? And ya'll actually have snow. I've never seen much of it."

"You say that like snow is a good thing." Elijah shuddered. "Well, welcome to Hobson Hill. I see Olive already gave you a welcome basket."

Carter looked back in it. "There's a hedgehog in

there." His coarse voice was getting rougher as he spoke. He wasn't used to talking so much. Doctors said it was good for him to do though.

"I put cider in there for you. It's in my favorite big girl cup, the one with Moana. There's also butter from Pooka and some of Daddy's bread. It's so yummy!"

"Thanks, Olive. I appreciate it," Carter said. The little girl still hung on his leg, smiling up at him. She was a cute one, he acknowledged, even though she was clearly a little crazy. It was a good crazy though.

"Your alpha won't mind me coming," Carter asked Elijah.

The man winced and lowered his eyes. "I don't have an Alpha, so no, that won't be a problem."

Carter was surprised. Happy, but surprised. This adorable man had to be beating them off with a stick. Of course, some folks thought poorly about single omegas, and some alphas refused to even speak to them. Idiots.

"I guess I'll see you tonight. What time?"

"Oh, is six okay?" Elijah's confidence seemed to bounce back at Carter's question.

"That's fine. I better get to work."

"Yes, of course," Elijah said and pulled Olive off Carter's leg. "Come on, Olive. We better get back to the house. We need to get you to school."

"Okay. Bye, Carter, love you!" The little girl and her dog ran off through the orchard.

"I swear it's exhausting keeping up with her," Elijah sighed. Carter smiled and held the hedgehog out to him. "Thanks," he said, taking Hodges and smiling shyly. "See you tonight. Have a good day at work."

Carter stood frozen as he watched Elijah walk away. He was in trouble. Big, wonderful trouble.

Buy Here: My Book

EXCERPT

Excerpt from *The Guppy Prince,* book one in The Silver Isles.

Dover Rees floated in the deepest part of his creek, enjoying the rushing sound of the waterfall to his right. Sunlight filtered through the water, glinting off the deep blue of his guppy tail. His thin and delicate caudal fin spread out like an elegant fan, dancing through the warm water as he swayed.

His favorite smooth and colorful pebbles were strewn around below him, and he admired the shells he had collected and placed beside them. Dover breathed deeply and enjoyed the peace and quiet. No one mocked him or bossed him around. No one watched him with cold eyes and hidden smirks. *I wish I could stay here forever.*

Sudden movement beside him jarred him from his thoughts and he laughed when Chubber grabbed a bright pink stone in his small brown paws and swam away. Dover's otter friend liked to steal Dover's shinies then share them with him again later.

A brook trout swam past him and Dover debated grabbing it for an early lunch, but he wasn't too hungry yet. Lately, he'd been eating less and less, and he couldn't make himself care.

The quiet water around him hummed as Nami quickly swam to him. His best friend's guppy tail was a lovely pink pattern with black dots, and her short black hair floated around her head. The cat with a mermaid tail on her black tankini top made him smile. He loved her purr-maid shirts.

"Have you eaten today, Your Highness?" she asked.

Dover scowled. "Don't call me that."

"When you're acting like a pouting asswipe, that's what you get called." Nami wrapped her arms around him and settled her head on his shoulder. "What's wrong with you, Dover?"

Dover had no answer for her. All he knew was he felt empty inside and it was harder and harder to get up in the morning. "I think I ate some bad clams."

"Every day for the past two months?" Nami leaned back and glared at him, her dark eyes seeing right through him.

Chubber came to his rescue, swimming in between them and wrapping his lean body across Dover's shoulders. "Chubber wants to get a snack."

Nami sighed, bubbles filling the water around her. "Mom is in your cottage making lunch. You're worrying us, bluetail."

Dover stroked a hand through her hair, then shoved

her down and pushed up, swimming toward the surface.

"Damn it!" Nami swam after him.

He laughed, heart warming. *Someone cares about me.* It wasn't his family, but Nami and her mom were closer to him than his parents or any of his twelve siblings.

Chubber clung to his back and nibbled on his ear until he mentally apologized. Chubber cared about him the most.

His creek was deep, but it didn't take him long to reach the surface. Shauna waited for them on the shore, hands on her hips. Chubber's mother, Shell, stood on her hind legs beside the mermaid, chirping loudly. Uh oh. He really was in trouble.

"You didn't eat breakfast, did you?" The wind blew strands of Shauna's pink hair across her face, ruining her glare.

"Sorry, Shauna."

She sighed. "I made your favorite."

"Grilled shrimp salad?" Dover's stomach rumbled.

"With avocado, papaya, mango, and pineapple. All your favorites." Shauna gave him a soft look. "Come eat, bluetail."

Dover summoned his human legs and a few seconds later, walked out of the creek, naked, with Chubber clinging to his shoulder. Shauna handed him a deep teal sarong, and he tied it about his waist.

Shell crawled up his leg and into his arms, then rubbed her slick furry face against his. She was a bit heavier than Chubber, but he was still a baby.

"Why does he get all the loving?" Nami asked, grumbling as she tied a sarong around her own waist.

Dover chuckled when Shauna arched an eyebrow at her daughter. "Did you say something, sweetness?"

"No, ma'am," Nami said, wincing.

"You two come eat lunch." Shauna turned around and walked toward Dover's large cottage.

Dover closed his eyes for a moment and savored the feel of the moss-covered rocks under his feet, and the comfortable breeze quickly drying his curly blue hair. He loved his home so much. It was his sanctuary.

Buy Here: https://amzn.to/2q9Q8en

www.ingramcontent.com/pod-product-compliance
Lightning Source LLC
Chambersburg PA
CBHW071741190726
48292CB00003B/838